SARANG

Other titles by Roger A. Caras
available in Bison Book Editions

THE CUSTER WOLF
Biography of an American Renegade

THE FOREST

MONARCH OF DEADMAN BAY
The Life and Death of a Kodiak Bear

PANTHER!

SOCKEYE
The Life of a Pacific Salmon

a novel

SARANG

THE STORY OF A BENGAL TIGER AND OF TWO CHILDREN IN SEARCH OF A MIRACLE

by ROGER A. CARAS

University of Nebraska Press • Lincoln

First Bison Book printing: 1991
Most recent printing indicated by the last digit below:
10   9   8   7   6   5   4   3   2   1

Library of Congress Cataloging-in-Publication Data
Caras, Roger A.
Sarang: the story of a Bengal tiger and of two children in search of a
miracle: a novel / by Roger A. Caras.
p.   cm.
ISBN 0-8032-6341-4 (pbk.)
1. Tigers—Fiction.   I. Title.
PS3553.A64S27   1991
813'.54—dc20
91-13128   CIP

Reprinted by arrangement with Roger A. Caras

♾

For My Mother

CONTENTS

CONTENTS

CONTENTS

SARANG

1

Dacca Recalled

There were dreams that went with the fever, recurring dreams, and although not all of them were nightmares in the classic sense, they were oppressive. When her temperature passed one hundred and four Liz's ears had started to ring, whine really, and she began slipping off to sleep for short intervals. But there was no rest in her sleep and she moved uneasily and called out angrily, "I didn't want to come. I told you that, Glenn. I told you something would happen if we did. We don't belong here." And then she would become quiet again and he would watch

3

her as she lay still and pale, breathing noisily through her open mouth. Every time she would sigh or twitch he would feel a wave of terror, a sickening feeling of helplessness come over him. He would wring out a towel from the bucket of cold well water that Raanaa, the house boy, kept replenishing, and gently mop her face and arms and legs. It was one of the few times that Glenn had ever felt guilty, really guilty, and he hated himself, he hated the hunting lodge, he hated the jungle and Pukmaranpur and the Gamalbuk River and Pakistan. He hated them all as much as he loved Liz. And in his hours of deepest concern Glenn's loves and hates fed off each other.

In administering the medication he followed the written instructions Dr. Hantman had given him. Chloroquin, a half a gram twice a day; tetracycline, two hundred and fifty milligrams six times a day; and ten grams of aspirin every three hours. Even with the drugs Liz's fever had lasted three days and he could see that she was losing weight. The dry, translucent pallor of her skin frightened him and he told himself over and over again that if anything happened to her he would never be able to forgive himself. She hadn't wanted to come, she hadn't wanted to leave Wichita. Pamela was ten now and Liz had felt that it was wrong for them to uproot the whole family for a year and disappear into the jungle. He reminded himself of that for the hundredth time as

4

he carefully pressed the cold towel to her forehead, her neck, her shoulders and breasts. She sighed and mumbled incoherently about thatched roofs harboring snakes, and tossed again recoiling from something she had seen in her dream.

Glenn hadn't slept in forty hours and the temperature in the valley was over a hundred. The cool breeze that had been drifting up the river from the lake had died several hours earlier and both the heat and the humidity had been climbing steadily. The heavy tropical vegetation that cascaded in billows of a thousand shades of green all around them seemed to shed heat and moisture and rot. In the thatch overhead lizards hunted for insects and the soft rustling of their passage provided a constant background murmur. He looked longingly at the empty bed a few feet away from Liz's and acknowledged realistically that he couldn't possibly last any longer. He took a prophylactic dose of chloroquin, dabbed sleepily at Liz's forehead once more and collapsed onto the empty bed. He managed to flick one shoe off but was dozing before he could hook his toe into the counter of the other. And then he, too, dreamed, fitfully, half-asleep, recalling in exquisite detail their departure from Kansas, the hectic, detail-laden stops in Washington and New York, the change of planes in London, the airport in Rome with all the leather goods in the gift shop and the postcards with the pictures of the Pope . . .

The 727 banked sharply to the right and began its approach to the airfield at Dacca in a long, low sweep over the rich delta lands of central East Pakistan. As the plane lost altitude the rice fields surrounding the villages glistened like gray mirrors in the slanting rays of the afternoon sun. Around their perimeters the low foliage darkened from pea to hunter's green. Men plodding behind their bullock carts didn't bother to look up. The mystery of the planes in which they would never fly was an old one to them now. The men, women and children who thundered overhead belonged to another century. If they were not to be envied they were to be ignored. Envy in Asia is a luxury few dare afford.

Glenn sat up abruptly when he heard the thud of the landing gear locking into place. As much as he had flown over the past years he was still a *listener* — a checker of aircraft sounds. In conversations with fellow passengers he had determined that most people are. Liz and Pamela didn't wake up until after the pilot had slipped the plane onto the concrete strip and the three jet engines began their screaming protest at being reversed against the wind. The plane taxied to the terminal. Another flight over and survived, he thought with relief.

Since they had cleared customs and immigrations back in Karachi, in arid, brutally hot, Urdu-speaking West Pakistan, the formalities at the airport

6

were mercifully brief. There were a number of hands to be shaken, a few photographs for which smiles had to be mustered, and then Glenn and his family were off for the hotel. In a matter of minutes they had dropped from the glaring blue and white sterility of the sky into the sweltering confusion of tropical Asia, from one century into another.

It wasn't until they were in the car heading into downtown Dacca that Glenn really had a chance to look at the man who had greeted him as the official government liaison man assigned to the project. He was strikingly handsome, in his mid-thirties, Glenn guessed. The deep brown skin and the slightly oriental cast to his features placed him as a Bengali, a man of the East, of the northeast of what once had been British India.

"Look, I'm sorry, but with all that going on at the airport I'm afraid . . ."

His host smiled warmly, and interrupted him.

". . . You didn't get my name. You don't speak Bengali?"

Glenn shook his head.

"Urdu?"

"I'm afraid not. Just English, American and some high school Spanish."

His host laughed easily and handed him a small, neat business card with Bengali script on one side and English on the other.

"Ata-ur Mohammed Khan."

"Not too bad for a foreigner. But, that's *'Hchahn'* not *'Kahn.'* You must get that *'Hch'* in there."

"Don't you have a short version?"

"Short version?"

"Yes. What do your friends call you? My name is Glenn Harvey Barclay. My friends call me Glenn."

His host went on to explain some of the vagaries of the Bengali language and assured him that he could call him either Ata or Khan without a breach of etiquette. Glenn, accustomed to reacting quickly to people, liked Ata more and more as they talked. He appeared to be a completely open person with none of the vague, reserved qualities that an American so often encounters overseas, where the expectancy that he will err is high. He was particularly pleased, therefore, to learn that Ata was going back into the Chittagong Hill Tracts with them. The self-consciousness that had prevailed on both sides when he met with the officials in Karachi just didn't seem to exist with Ata. He began to understand the apparent difference when Ata explained that he had gone to a British military academy in Lahore and then to university in London for three years. This guy's as Western as I am, he thought, only he's Eastern too. It must be a tough combination to live with. He thought of the four weeks he and Liz had spent in London at a World Food conference three years earlier and then looked out of the window as Dacca slipped past and around them. How does one guy belong to both of these worlds, he wondered, and still know who he is?

The driver of the ancient Chevy leaned heavily on the horn as they worked their way through a market area. Pink, lavender, silver, green and gold rickshaws on the backs of bicycles; bullock carts, cattle, goats and sheep jammed up ahead, mingling with thousands of people on foot. Liz covered her eyes as they were hurtled into a great mass of people and animals with no reduction in speed. Wholesale slaughter seemed imminent.

Suddenly Pamela, who had been staring out the window in quiet fascination, reacted.

"Daddy! Mummy! Look over there! A stage-coach!"

"Oh, from your cowboy films. Yes, we still use them. If you like contrasts, that building behind it is the Atomic Energy Authority. You Westerners seem to have a great fondness for our contrasts."

And there were striking contrasts to engage the three Americans. Sleek racing horses were being led down the street by their bare-footed grooms past ugly diminutive, thin-legged horses pulling overburdened carts. Both horses and wagons looked as if they would collapse at any moment. Mercedes sedans shot by bullock carts, their horns blaring.

9

Well-dressed college students pedaled furiously on their bicycles heading for the evening book market, skirting peasants squatting by the side of the road with their begging bowls, ready to harass the first pedestrian who didn't give them a wide enough berth.

The driver had to brake to a complete stop a number of times when obstacles loomed up that would not be moved with the insistent bleat of the horn. On one occasion a herd of black milk cows, their dung-matted bodies hanging like giant sacks on protruding hip and shoulder bones, was driven out across the road, blocking it completely. While the driver leaned on the horn Liz studied the pressing crowd surrounding the car. She was stunned by the sight of a little girl — she estimated her to be no more than four — holding out a begging bowl and pleading in a soft, chanting whine to the indifferent crowd that surged around her. The child was filthy and covered with sores. At her feet an old man, naked except for a brief cloth, lay on a pallet of dirty rags. His bones protruded so much that his knees and elbows looked like massive swellings. He stretched a skeletal hand with bulging knuckles toward the crowd which ignored him as it did the girl. His eyes were so deeply sunken into his head that Liz couldn't see them. Together the two, the old man and the little girl, looked like the decaying remnants of what had once been human beings. They looked as if they had been resurrected from hell itself. Liz closed her eyes, took a deep breath, and looked again. Glenn saw them, too, but he was watching his wife. He was confused by the fact that he felt worse for her than for them.

"Ata! Those people, that man and that baby! My God, what's wrong with them? It's horrible! Just horrible!"

Ata looked embarrassed and just shrugged. Liz knew immediately that she had chosen the wrong sight to comment on and thought briefly about apologizing but decided against it. She sank down into the seat as far as she could and refused to look out of the window for the rest of the trip. She hugged Pamela to her and fought back the terrible feeling of nausea that welled up within her. She felt mounting resentment at her own feelings of guilt for having commented on the horror she had witnessed. Why the devil shouldn't I have said something, she thought, those people are dying a horrible death out there and here we're all comfortable and concerned with social niceties. What the hell are we doing here anyway? She was near tears as the car swung in an arc through the gates onto the hotel grounds and several uniformed servants scurried forward to open the doors for them.

The Intercontinental Hotel took them by surprise. It was slick, polished, ultramodern in every respect, and a blessed wave of clean, cool air flowed over them as they entered the lobby. Smartly uniformed bellhops greeted them one by one as they moved across the lobby to the registration desk. Each bowed as they passed and said in perfect English, "Good afternoon sir, madame, miss." Pamela was fascinated, for most of them appeared to be no older than herself.

After Glenn had finished with the registration formalities and been reassured with the promise that their passports would be returned in the morning, they were shown to their spacious, modern suite. The arrangement for Ata to return in two hours to take them to dinner left them time to unpack and wash away the dust of West Pakistan. Glenn stopped to tip the four bellhops who had scrambled to their service in the lobby. He could hear the tubs being drawn in both bathrooms and with practical resignation settled down to the business of unpacking rumpled clothes and making a few entries in his expense diary.

He paused briefly as he moved past the big picture window overlooking the broad avenue that ran by the front of the hotel. Far below, beyond the reach of the air conditioning, out of sight of the flowered drapes and the chrome and rosewood furniture, an infuriated farmer was lashing two enormous white bullocks as they labored to move his grossly overladen cart of produce down toward the market. They strained against the excessive weight and the inefficiency of badly worn wooden wheels like two somnambulant giants doing their time in purgatory. Several grotesquely crippled beggars squatted at the gates of the hotel grounds eyeing the tall, bearded doorman in his shocking-pink turban who forced them to keep their distance. A black Chrysler flying a consular flag swept into the drive, forcing one of the mendicants to leap aside. He crawled and tumbled across the drive entrance like a distorted spider. Glenn shook his head, wondering if Liz had been right. Ever since Karachi he had been questioning his own wisdom in accepting this assignment. Perhaps an American family from Kansas didn't belong in tropical Asia. He thought about it and went back to unpacking.

"Listen, before we go down to meet Ata I think we should get something straight."

Liz dropped her eyes and then looked up at Glenn.

"I've been waiting for this. I know, I goofed in the car. I'm sorry, it just came out. I've never seen human beings look like that before. It was horrible!"

"I know it was horrible, but we were warned at the briefing session at the U.N. — and don't forget the lecture we got at the State Department. We just can't start off by criticizing things we don't like."

"My God, Glenn! It's not a matter of not liking something. It's just a matter of being human and having human emotions!"

"Honey! What good did you do those poor devils

by embarrassing Ata in front of Pamela and me? Here's a perfectly nice guy whom you've known for ten minutes. You're driving through his home town, past new buildings, a college, some great old monuments and your one observation is that there is poverty. Now how the devil do you think that made him feel? Do you suppose he likes seeing that kind of thing in his own country? Look, we're going to be seeing an awful lot of things that don't look like Wichita. This place just isn't like home! People still starve to death in Asia, sometimes by the millions. That's why we're here, remember? To help, not to comment. Save the comments for your letters to your sister. Okay?"

Liz liked the way Glenn scolded her, although she would never admit it. It was gentle but firm and it reminded her of her father's sensible way of disciplining his six children on their Kansas farm, a long time ago, a long way away. She looked at Glenn for a long minute. She knew from experience that the tone for the rest of the evening would be set by the way she took his reprimand. She decided that this wasn't the time to give him one of her periodic reminders that she was all female through and through.

"It won't happen again. I promise."

They walked down the hall and caught up with Pamela, who had gone ahead to ring for the elevator. They both smiled when they found her explaining her charm bracelet to the young elevator boy. Liz squeezed Glenn's hand.

"There's at least one of us who's not going to have any trouble."

"Trouble doing what, Mummy?"

"Trouble jumping over the moon."

"Daddy! You promised not to give me those silly answers!"

The elevator arrived at the lobby and as they stepped out they spotted Ata waiting for them near the great glass doors. Somehow, Glenn felt as if they had reached the point of no return. They could either retreat into the elevator, pack their bags and escape, or go forward into whatever trouble and difficulties lay ahead. Ata, standing there waiting, seemed to challenge them, to dare them to see it through . . .

Glenn heard Liz mumble, he heard her turn in her sleep and he hung for a moment, suspended, not certain if he was dreaming. He thought he asked her if she wanted to go home but later he wouldn't be sure, he wouldn't be able to recall whether he had asked her in the hotel lobby in Dacca, in the hunting lodge at Pukmaranpur in the midst of her fever, or not at all.

He listened, only half awake, and heard her re-

assuringly steady breathing. Then he wondered if it was his own he heard. As the damp stain of sweat spread out on the sheet beneath him he stopped wondering and slipped effortlessly back into his dream of recall.

2

The Challenge

Dinner in the hotel's plush dining room went very well, except for Liz's second big mistake of the day. She launched into a curry with a little too much enthusiasm and gulped down a tumbler of water before Ata could stop her. The water only made the burning worse and Ata saved her life, she later assured him, when he ordered a bunch of finger bananas brought on the double.

Under Ata's watchful eyes she ate three of the bananas, each no bigger than her husband's thumb, and the terrible sensation that the roof of her mouth

17

was peeling away slowly faded. She looked up to see a group of waiters standing off to the side grinning knowingly and managed a wan smile. The curry was removed and a platter of fresh mango slices lying on a bed of crushed ice was substituted. All in all, it was a pleasant dinner, but Liz was tired from the long trip and the time-changes. She was glad when it was Pamela's bedtime and she had a valid reason for excusing herself.

Ata stood to shake her hand and instinctively she knew the time was right.

"Ata. Forgive us our trespasses . . ."

Her host smiled, and to her surprise, added:

"Even as we forgive those who trespass against us."

"You know the Lord's Prayer!"

"I'm very interested in Christianity. It's a fascinating study. Please don't ask me to forgive you for your humanity, Mrs. Barclay. I hope you will come to know in time that we have ours in Asia despite our problems of survival. Goodnight."

Glenn and Ata watched Liz and Pamela work their way out between the tables and leave the dining room past a row of bowing waiters and maitre d's.

"I believe I know what you're thinking, Glenn. Don't worry. They'll be fine."

"I hope so, Ata, I hope so. They're a long way from home."

Glenn sensed that the first session with Ata

should be introductory, on the personal level. The conversation drifted from family to education to general interests, and only after an hour to specifics.

The choice of Glenn H. Barclay, agricultural consultant, by the Food Commission at the United Nations had been a last-minute decision. By the time he had been able to clear up his obligations to his firm in Kansas and get through the indoctrination at the State Department in Washington there had been only a few days left for meetings in the great glass building overlooking the East River from Manhattan. He was painfully aware of his own ignorance and was hoping that Ata would volunteer a great deal of the information he needed.

"What did they tell you in New York about the Chittagong Hill Tract peoples?"

"Not as much as I would have liked. Can you fill me in on the details?"

Ata gave him a quick run-down on the challenge he faced. Glenn was very attentive and saved his questions until the end.

The Chittagong Hill Tract peoples are the tribal groups, Ata explained, that inhabit the southeastern region of East Pakistan, bordering on Burma and India's Assam State. He went on to describe the six tribes and their different levels of cultural attainment. At the top are the Chakmas, a sophisticated tribe that will probably disintegrate in the next few decades as the younger people seek out the cities and are absorbed. Just below them are the Mugg peoples. Descending from them in the social scale are the Kukkees, Maroongs, Kumis, and the Banujogis. The latter are a deep-jungle people living in almost complete nudity far removed from the mainstream of Asiatic progress. Glenn's special problem was the Mugg village of Pukmaranpur.

"What really happened there? All I got was a few scattered details."

"In a way it's rather typical, I'm afraid. We had a very eager young politician who got himself assigned to the U.N. Mission and let his enthusiasm run away with his good sense. He got involved with the agricultural authorities there and somehow they worked out a crazy scheme to elevate the economic level of Pukmaranpur in a crash program of modernization. It was to be a model village. They forgot that the inhabitants are only people and that they can't move two hundred years in six weeks, even with tractors."

Ata went on to explain the sudden appearance of the twelve agricultural experts in the village, with the photographers right behind them. The big barges appeared a few days later, sputtering up the small jungle tributary from Lake Karnaphuli, loaded with crates and boxes.

The pipes were laid into the river, the pumps installed, and water was flowing into the irrigation ditches within the first week. Tractors were assembled and local farmers given a rudimentary training program in their use. Diesel fuel was moved in in fifty-gallon drums, an electricity generator was installed, and in less than a month you couldn't hear the birds for the machinery. Groups of bewildered villagers were ushered into line beside the tractors and ordered to smile for the photographers.

The program went off without trouble and in groups of two and three the experts were withdrawn. Finally, the villagers lined up along the banks of their river to watch the last of the politicians and minor officials depart. The people of Pukmaranpur were left with all the symbols of the twentieth century and none of the traditions that make the evolution and application of technology possible.

"What happened after the aggie team left?"

"Just what you might expect. The equipment began breaking down."

The picture Ata painted was both predictable and ironic. No one in the village had had any technological background. They were scared to death of the monsters left in their care. One man, probably the only really mechanically inclined villager who had been given any training, was badly scalded when a tractor radiator blew its top. He refused to go near the equipment after that and the other drivers decided it would be safer not to fill the radiators at all since all they appeared to do was generate unwanted heat and steam. Replacement parts were not properly protected from the rain and rust, and mildew set in. In a matter of two months most of the equipment was out of commission and the peasant farmers were making up for lost time by working their fields in the way they had always been worked, by hand.

"How long has it been since you were up there?"

"Just a month. Except for a few signs here and there you would hardly know anything had happened. One tractor, the only one the jungle hasn't overgrown completely, has a banana tree growing up out of the radiator. An old man collected a basketful of flash-bulbs and film canisters and left them as an offering at the Buddhist shrine, along with a basket of fruit and flowers."

Glenn shook his head and stared down at the parallel lines he had been unconsciously inscribing in the table cloth with his fork. It was the same old story — well-intentioned people, always in a hurry, crashing in on a compact and functioning culture, trying to superimpose a whole network of foreign elements on a bewildered people, on a strict timetable.

"You see, those people didn't feel underprivileged. They thought they were happy. Now, of course, they don't know."

"But they are working at a pretty low level of efficiency, Ata. They're not getting back anywhere near enough for the labor they put in."

"But they don't know that's bad, Glenn. They've never seen a wheat field in Kansas and a picture of one doesn't mean any more to them than the jets they hear flying overhead at thirty thousand feet."

"Ata. Will you level with me?"

"Level with you? That must be American, it's not English."

"Yes, it's American. Will you be completely honest with me? On the line?"

"Of course."

"You're against my experiments too, aren't you? You think I should pack up and go home and leave Pukmaranpur alone!"

Ata looked at him carefully. Glenn wasn't being accusing — he was just asking a completely open, honest question. How different they are from the English, Ata thought, how really completely different. Everything head-on without style or subterfuge.

"No. I'm not against your plan. I just wonder if you know what you're doing, that's all."

"Oh, I can answer that for you. I don't. I don't know a damn thing about elephants, but those people up there on that river do. Elephants have been used in those forests for two thousand years. There's a tradition for them, and the people can understand them where they might not savvy a tractor. I'm not going up there with any great secret to divulge. I'm going up there to use that village as a laboratory, and maybe, just maybe, do some good along the way. I want to see if elephants can be used for something besides logging and holy processions. A big elephant can put out a lot of power — horsepower, if you want — and he can be maintained on local fodder. The breeding potential is good, they live a long time, and they don't need spare parts. That's it. It's an experiment."

"Do you have adequate financial backing for this scheme?"

"U.N. activities are never adequately financed. My budget is small, unrealistically small perhaps, but it's what was available and what I have to work with. We'll make out."

"May I ask you a blunt question?"

"Shoot."

"Why did they send you? There are a lot of elephant people in the world, even a lot of zoo people who understand these beasts, and they're tricky, believe me. You're a horse and cow man. Why *you*?"

Glenn looked at Ata and smiled. Ata was smiling, too, even before he answered.

"You know, Ata old boy, I've been asking myself that same question halfway around the world. Why me?"

3

Beyond Chittagong

The flight on the twin-engined Fokker Friendship from Dacca to Chittagong took forty minutes. There were no formalities at the small airport and within twenty minutes after landing they had loaded themselves and their luggage into the waiting Volkswagen Microbus and were heading out past the docks toward the Kaptai Road. Their driver threaded through the dense crowds moving along the high embankment that overlooked the harbor. Glenn marveled at the variety of ships bunched up against every available foot of dock space. Out in the roadstead other ships waited their turn. The less patient were being off-loaded onto barges by near-naked laborers glistening like bronze that had learned how to sweat. Merchantmen newly from the ways in Japan and proud of their paint nudged perilously close to rusted hulks with fifty years and more of service in Asian waters. Chittagong, East Pakistan's one big port, huddling on the eastern shore of the Bay of Bengal, was as it has always been: frenetic, hot, chaotic, yet somehow beautiful because of its surging vitality. Glenn wondered what Kipling had felt the first time he was pedaled across this same causeway in his garishly painted rickshaw.

An ancient bridge on the outskirts of Chittagong had grown tired and collapsed and the driver was forced to take an additional leg to the north through Pahartali before he could make any progress toward the east. It was another hour before they were on the good two-lane blacktop running to Lake Karnaphuli. A soft, cooling breeze blew across the rich rice fields that bordered the road on both sides as far as they could see. Clumps and intersecting avenues of palms broke the monotony and there were endless streams of livestock along the road and bathing in roadside ditches. Periodically the derelict ruin of an ancient temple testified to the long history of the land.

They stopped halfway to Kaptai to get cold drinks from the icebox that was crammed in, with their luggage, behind the back seat. Glenn wandered over to the edge of the road, beer can in hand, and stared down into the fields that fell away from his feet.

At the foot of the causeway on which the road was laid there was a deep ditch no more than a few dozen feet wide. Water plants lined the banks and blue, spiky flowers stood like miniature soldiers knee-deep in the brown water. Beyond the low dike that bordered the ditch the soft green rice fields began, laced geometrically with ribbons of water that repeated the pattern of the sky. Men, women and children bent over double at the work of planting moved forward in slow cadence, their rapidly working hands alone indicating the urgency of their task. To his right the ditch opened into a small pond where a group of fishermen, standing chest-deep in the muddy water, were casting circular nets in low, gentle arcs. Water droplets glistened in the sun as the nets sailed through the air, and it looked as if the men were playing some strange ballet-like game with silver cloth. Somewhere, out of sight, a man was chanting, humming, propitiating. From the left a herdsman was moving his cattle along the shallow shelf on the far side of the ditch. Knee-deep the cattle ploughed along, obedient to the soft melodic commands of the man behind them.

Glenn slipped down the embankment to be on a

level with the cows when they came abreast as he waved to the herdsman. The muscular young man broke into a broad grin and raised his hand in greeting. He called out but Glenn couldn't grasp the meaning of what was obviously a question. He shrugged at the man and smiled.

"He wants to know if you are interested in cattle."

Glenn turned and looked up. Ata was standing on the top of the embankment looking down at him.

"Tell him I am . . . please."

Ata called to the man in Bengali and without hesitation the herdsman tapped a large cow on the rump with his stick and herded her into the ditch. Jumping in after her he grabbed her by the horn and they swam across together. Cow and man scrambled up the muddy bank at Glenn's feet, the man still smiling broadly.

Instinctively Glenn extended his hand and the man accepted it after saluting. He ran his hands over the flanks of the dripping cow and squatted down to examine her udder. The herdsman stood over him beaming. When Glenn stood he realized for the first time the size of the herdsman. Although extremely muscular, he was not over five foot six. Glenn towered over him and felt exaggerated and self-conscious. It was a one-sided awkwardness, however, for the herdsman was still beaming with pride at the visitor who had taken an interest in his possession. Looking down Glenn noticed three leeches attached to the man's left leg. The herdsman followed the line of his gaze and without any discernible reaction flicked them off with the big toe of his other foot. The smile never left his face.

Glenn was suddenly faced with the problem of thanking the man for his trouble, complimenting him on his cows and taking his leave. He realized with more than a slight feeling of frustration that he didn't know a single word that would communicate any of his thoughts. But there is a universal language, and it is heard with the eyes. He patted the cow, nodding appreciatively to the man, and smiled, saluting as the man had done before extending his hand. The herdsman laughed softly, musically, patted the cow in imitation and accepted Glenn's hand. It was then that Glenn realized that he had actually made a friend, a friend who would take him home, introduce him to his family, share his meager food supply with him — and yet no words had been spoken. He felt for the first time that he was seeing the face of Pakistan he would have to come to know. Before the elephants there would be people.

No two people react the same way to a time and a place no matter how closely they seem to be related in earlier shared experiences. For Liz the trip was more difficult than it was for either her husband or her daughter. Each mile took her farther away from the security of knowing she could cope with anything that might happen. Each mile was a mile deeper into the unknown about herself. Nothing was familiar, nothing reminded her of previous problems or previous solutions. It was an uncertain trip and barely missed plunging her into a fit of depression. She kept telling herself that she would cope, she would still manage to be the good wife and the good mother, the two qualities that justified her existence to herself and on which her fierce, farm-bred pride was founded. The Earth-Mother, Glenn called her, and the Earth-Mother she was. But then she would look out of the window and see the strange dark faces that swept by them as they flew down the straightaways, and she would doubt herself again. Her entire childhood had been spent in preparation for the role she had played so well since her marriage at the age of eighteen. She cooked well before she was twelve, and she was making her own dresses, at least her everyday school dresses, by the time she was fourteen. She had even been able to splint Glenn's broken leg when he fell out of a tree on the camping trip they took in Yosemite on their honeymoon. Liz's efficiency, her ability to fulfill her destiny of wife and homemaker, was the footing on which her sense of self was based. She knew by instinct that if she ever failed in her chosen role her whole sense of self-worth would crumble. Consciously she feared the uncertainty of her new, totally strange environment be-cause it threatened to make her inadequate. And for Liz, Liz of the farm, Liz of Kansas and the make-do philosophy, life was one long struggle against the paramount sin of inadequacy.

Pamela was never without a sense of wonder. In her almost eleven years she had moved from one great adventure into another and was usually far too involved with the moment to be very nostalgic about the past or too concerned about the future. Not yet a teen-ager, and with only the earliest signs of the pre-teen-ager's rebellious nature, she could swing in minutes from full-blown joy to overwhelming sorrow. Total retreat and quick repair were always available in the arms of either parent. Laughter and tears were instant and easy, intense absorption was the hallmark of each new experience.

For Pamela the trip across southeastern Pakistan toward the Burmese border was a kaleidoscope. From the blistering heat, the dust and the noise of Karachi, tropical Dacca had been a nap away. From Dacca to Chittagong had been less than two chapters' worth of *Black Beauty*, and the run from the frantic port facilities of Chittagong to the flat green country along the Kaptai Road had been an end-lessly changing panorama of colors, animals, and new faces. Each roadside market they passed of-fered new sounds, new sights, and new smells. The fruits and vegetables piled up on wicker trays were unrecognizable, and the streams of adults and children walking beside the road with loads of produce on their heads interested her intensely. Perhaps more than either of her parents, Pamela had arrived in East Pakistan. Untroubled by any of their uncertainties and safe from self-doubt, she was absorbing, sensing, feeling the time and the place. There was no wall over which she had to climb to enter the new fields beyond. She was already there and as committed to living each moment to its fullest as she had always been.

Beyond Chandraghona the Barclay family barely missed being involved in a tragedy. On the outskirts of the town there was a small market and several garishly painted produce trucks were pulled off beside the road. As they came abreast of one green, purple and red truck, painted with slogans and endless garlands of imaginary flowers, the cab door flew open and a boy of about six dropped into the road directly in front of the Volkswagen. The driver reacted immediately and swerved just in time to avoid him. The Microbus plowed into a mass of fruit and vegetables heaped on mats under an awning in front of a shack. An old man was just able to roll out of the way in time. Although a lot of produce was squashed, no one was injured. While an irate father soundly pummeled the screaming child a crowd gathered to discuss the damage done and the tragedy averted. There was no open hostility and Ata was able to settle on a figure with the old man without too much trouble. The bill paid, the old man insisted that they share tea with him and as the crowd drifted off they sat on mats beside the Volkswagen and drank the steaming black liquid from earthenware cups. The old man's relatives arrived from several different directions and it was an hour before Ata was able to get his charges away from the market and back onto the road to Kaptai. They carried a fresh supply of mangoes and bananas with them and one enormous jackfruit the size of a football that Ata assured them they would not like. He was right, and the coarse pulpy fruit was abandoned by the roadside in favor of the bananas, which were sweeter and more intensely flavorful than any they had ever tasted before.

A guard at the tollgate outside Kaptai asked them to keep their cameras undercover while in the town and not to linger long near any of the structures that were a part of the hydroelectric project there. Noting with satisfaction that the project had been engineered by a firm from Salt Lake City, they passed quickly through the restricted area, were relieved of the government passes without which they could not have entered the town at all, and arrived at the shores of Lake Karnaphuli. The vast, blue, amoeba-shaped lake spread out to the north, the south, and the east. None of its distant shores was in sight. As their blue and white motor launch slipped free of the pier and was guided to the north, Ata joined Glenn and Liz at the rail.

"We'll pass Rangamati on the west bank in a couple of hours," Ata said. "After that you're in tribal country. If you keep your eyes open you might see some wild elephant. You can sometimes see them coming down to bathe."

The uncertainty Liz had felt earlier in the day was reduced somewhat by the new setting. This moving across the broad, blue lake, the cool breeze that renewed the air, these were more familiar than the bazaars and rice fields had been. As a tourist Liz would have enjoyed and been fascinated by everything they had seen, everything they had smelled and tasted. But she was not a tourist. She was expected to create a home in a sea of strangeness and she was afraid of being submerged. The fact that she came from stock that had faced the same problem in Kansas didn't seem to be helping her as much as she had thought it would when she had worried about it in advance.

For Glenn, the mention of wild elephants suddenly put everything into focus. He had arrived, and the anticipation and the private self-doubts were behind him. He could no longer indulge in such luxuries. His private strength lay in his fierce determination never to give up until every conceivable ounce of energy and imagination had been expended and he suddenly felt at ease. He always did just before the battle began. He looked out across the lake, then along the deck of the launch. He shook his head and smiled as he saw Pamela sitting on top of a crate trying to explain her charm bracelet to the launch owner's son.

4

The River

Glenn pitched and turned. His pillow had fallen on the floor and a large dark stain showed where his head had been. He could hear Liz muttering and groaning somewhere far off and he thought briefly of going to look for her. But he was absorbed by the adventure he was reliving. He twisted over again and let his arms flop down on either side of the narrow cot as he let Liz slip away.

The blue and white motor launch continued on a northward tack well out in the lake after passing

Rangamati on the port beam. After three eventless hours it began edging in toward the bank. The captain, a tall, angular Bengalese of indeterminable age, picked his way through a narrow channel in a swampy area that bridged the gap between an overgrown island and the mainland. From a distance it looked like open water, but once the launch had entered the channel Glenn leaned over the rail and could see a few patches of sandy bottom between clumps of submerged weeds. In places the water was only inches deep and was so clogged with vegetation that it appeared to be solid ground. A snake couldn't get through that, he thought, not without a pilot.

Once the island fell away from the starboard beam the channel broadened and an avenue of clear, still water opened out into the lake beyond. They were done with open water, though, and the captain swung the launch over hard to port and slipped it in behind a curtain of vegetation. Dipping its ends in the water, the thick tangle hung down fifty feet from the towering trees that crowded the bank. They eased through the screen and faced up the Gamalbuk River. Although it was a narrow stream the launch resumed speed as they penetrated deep under the green arch that closed over their heads.

It was as if their launch had entered a tunnel, Liz commented. Despite her oppressive misgivings she had to acknowledge the strange, submerged beauty of the place as she moved up next to Glenn and rested her forearms on the rail. Almost immediately the jungle sounds began. There was a disturbance in the broad canopy that arched across the river and two pale brown monkeys burst out of the foliage with three others in hot pursuit.

"Macaques," Ata said as he moved up to the rail beside them.

Further off in the jungle, out of sight, there was a harsh, insistent cawing.

"Sounds like our crows back in Kansas," Glenn observed.

"That's what they are," Ata replied, "they're jungle crows. They're everywhere. We call them *kaak* after the noise they make."

In several places the stream widened and the launch moved at full speed across open pools. They passed the mouths of a number of feeder streams but generally the Gamalbuk was a narrow watery alley into a solid block of dense jungle. Several times they heard a crashing off behind the screen of vegetation.

"Are those elephants?"

"They could be. I don't know, though, it's a little thick in here for them. They're more likely wild boar or swamp deer. There might be some *sambar* in here, too. It's difficult to tell."

The river began twisting in a series of tortuous

turns and a number of small islands appeared midstream. In places the trees from both banks intermingled overhead with those growing on the islands so that the launch had the choice of two green tunnels. The humidity was high and the refreshing breeze from the lake was lost in the thick swamp.

The bird life along the river was endless in its variety. Liz spotted a beautiful green parrakeet with a rose-colored beak. It was sitting on a small branch overhanging the water. She raised her hand to point it out to Glenn and stared in disbelief as the tree exploded with parrakeets. At least two hundred of the swift-flying birds, trailing their long green and blue tails, burst out from what seemed to be every leaf. Their harsh screaming notes falling behind them, they were gone like a cluster of arrows shot into the forest. Before Liz could comment, two ashy-gray sarus cranes, five feet tall and with bright red heads, wandered out from behind a windfall and stood knee-deep near the bank, staring at the launch as it chugged past. There was something surrealistic about them. They had an air of disdain, as if they knew they had been designed by Brancusi and despised the ugly shapes that intruded themselves into their world.

"Glenn, have you ever seen such birds? They're magnificent!"

It was her first positive reaction and Glenn felt, for the first time really, that everything was going to be all right. But before he could answer, Liz grabbed his arm and pointed straight ahead. A large crocodile was sculling toward shore, barely visible except for its wake.

"*Koomeer*," Ata informed them, "they are feared. You must be careful near the water. I've never known anyone to be hurt by them but the villagers speak of it."

"That's the end of our swimming for this year," Liz said firmly.

Pamela joined them at the rail as the vegetation beside the river began to thin out. They could see light shining between the trees. Finally the enclosure opened up completely and a flat, grassy plain reached out toward another patch of jungle half a mile back from the river. More sarus cranes fed in pairs in the shallow water along the bank and a huge porcupine moved slowly along a fallen tree that lay a dozen feet back from the river. There was an arrogance about him that was testimony to his sense of security. He never hurried because he could never believe anything would have the temerity to molest him. A slight breeze blew across the open flat, offering a welcome relief from the stifling heat of the swamp. As the river took another turn to the right they could see forested hills rising up in the background six or seven miles away.

"Daddy, Mummy, look at those deer in the field. They're beautiful."

"They're *chital*, honey," Glenn explained, "the most beautiful deer in the world."

And beautiful they were. Three handsome stags, each three feet tall at the shoulder, stood watching while eleven does fed without concern a few dozen yards off. Their bright red-fawn coats glistened in the sun and the white spots that covered them in random fashion on top and in neat longitudinal rows below shone like little points of light. The bucks sported tall antlers that swept almost straight up with angular brow tines sticking out in front. They watched the launch pass without moving and then went back to feeding. The fear-corner of their collective herd brain was tuned to a different frequency, that of cat and stealth, of parting bushes and exploding shadows.

Although the jungle was still very much in evidence back from the river and on the slopes of the hills that now rose above them on both sides, the country along the banks was more open. The oppressive monotony of the tunnel through which they had sailed was relieved now by more and more variety. Here and there rocks could be seen and Glenn thought he saw several areas that looked as if they had been cultivated. Twice they passed logs floating downstream that had distinct axe marks, and at one point they passed a half-submerged, derelict pirogue resting at the water's edge. In order to skirt some debris that had piled up against an island midstream the launch pilot eased over to the left bank and slipped through a deep channel that he knew by experience would give him water under his keel.

As the launch moved along within a dozen feet of the open forest Liz peered in between the trees looking for more wildlife. Suddenly she grabbed her husband by the arm and fairly shrieked in his ear.

"Glenn! Elephants! I saw elephants."

Glenn spun to follow Liz's pointing finger and from between the trees a single elephant emerged. On his neck a *mahout* sat, one leg folded under him, the other pressed in behind the tuskless animal's huge ear. The man's casual appearance was emphasized by the black umbrella he held open over his head. He broke into a broad grin as Pamela waved to him and barked a single word of command to the elephant, who raised his trunk in a smart salute.

Glenn, the horse-and-cow man, moved back along the rail as the launch passed the elephant and the *mahout*, in order to keep them in sight as long as possible. He scarcely noticed Pamela, who hung on to his hand and shot questions at him faster than he could register them.

"Boy, I'm going to love working with them! Did you hear him give the order for that salute? A one word command, given once!" He turned to Ata, who had joined him at the stern with Liz.

"Was that a male, Ata?"

"A *makhna*. A tuskless male. They're quite common and make good workers although they're handicapped in stacking logs. We don't have too many good tuskers here in the hills."

"Ata, how do you tell a *makhna* from a lady elephant, without getting personal?"

"Practice, I guess. Some elephants look like males, and some look like females. The elephant catchers can tell by the way they stand, the way they walk, almost by the way they breathe. I'm not that good. I knew that one was a male because I know the *mahout*. His name is Satwyne."

"Whose name?" Glenn asked.

"The *mahout* was Satwyne. That elephant is Bolo Bahadur. *Bahadur* means brave. Bolo Bahadur is a famous *koonki*."

Pamela was very much involved in the conversation. "What's a *koonki*, Mr. Khan?"

Glenn noticed with satisfaction that Pamela got the pronunciation of *Khan* exactly right. It was without affectation, just right. She'll be speaking Bengali before I get my first elephant behind a plow, he thought, and smiled to himself.

"A *koonki* is an elephant that is trained to capture other elephants. It is dangerous and difficult work and a good *koonki* is a very valuable animal."

The discussion of elephant lore was cut short by increased activity up near the bow. The launch was rounding a bend and ahead of them on the left bank a group of thatched roofs could be seen under an enormous banyan tree.

"Pukmaranpur, Glenn. Welcome to your new home."

Glenn felt Liz move up beside him and reached over and took her hand. He turned slightly so he could watch her face and what he saw worried him. It was one of the few times since their marriage that he couldn't gauge her reactions. Her face was a blank, impassive, staring straight ahead. Even when his eyes caught hers and she turned to face him he couldn't penetrate her mask. Then, as she read the worried expression on his face, the corners of her mouth twitched and she smiled reassuringly. The bow of the launch nudged the riverbank and he caught her just as she was losing her balance. "It's okay, Glenn, it's okay just as long as we're all together."

5

Khoka

Pukmaranpur had grown up on the bank of the Gamalbuk River over many more generations than anyone could remember. A dozen of the village's thatched buildings overlooked the river itself but most of the thousand inhabitants lived in small clusters on three of the four hills within the village boundaries or on the edges of the broad valleys that the jungle had surrendered hundreds of years ago. The valleys were largely given over to rice paddies, while small, square, terraced fields on the hillsides provided room for secondary crops that required less water.

If there was a center to the village it was on the flat plaza in front of the Buddhist school. Paths led off from the plaza to the river, to the field complexes and to the clusters of individual huts that spread out over an area of about a square mile. The tallest of the village's four hills was topped by a Buddhist temple. Fifty-two worn stone steps led up the side of the steep knoll and through the saffron yellow arch with the silver finial and small, pointed metal flag. The courtyard beyond the archway had two branches, one leading to a statue of the Buddha set in a small stone building painted a deep navy blue, and the other to the statue of an ancient monk who long ago had ruled over the consciences of Pukmaranpur's ancestral inhabitants.

There was no organized system for keeping the village clean but somehow it remained reasonably neat and free from clutter. The hard-packed dirt trails that led from area to area were never littered, and the small plazas in front of the huts were swept regularly by the people who had to look out upon them. Many huts were surrounded by fences of reeds and sticks, and small gardens were maintained for household use. Banana, mango, papaya and jackfruit trees were evident everywhere and beyond the last cluster of huts pineapple fields spread out for a dozen acres. Near the edge of the village, along the river, a small mosque stood on a flat open rise, and a Hindu shrine was tucked back into a glade a thousand yards inland. God had learned to answer to many names in Pukmaranpur.

Some tethered cattle, a few dozen goats and a scattering of nondescript leggy chickens wandered freely between the huts, but the number of head of stock was surprisingly small for an agricultural settlement of a thousand people. Some of this Glenn noted as Ata led them across the plaza in front of the school to the long thatched building that served a variety of community needs.

The seven village elders rose as Liz, Pamela, Glenn and Ata ducked through the low doorway. They're very Western, Glenn thought, as the elders shook hands all around and indicated seats for the visitors. Ata explained that his wards did not speak Bengali or any of the hill dialects, and to Glenn's overwhelming relief two of the elders announced that they spoke English.

Bowls of fresh fruit were brought in and passed around. The atmopshere was hospitable, even friendly. Glenn had feared that their initial reception might be stiff and awkward, and was relieved more for Liz and Pamela's sake than his own.

Liz relaxed somewhat when the two old men sitting nearest to her laughed aloud at the mess she was making with her pineapple. It was richer in flavor and far juicier than any she had ever tasted, and try as she would she couldn't take a bite without having rivers of nectar flow down over her chin. When she looked down and saw the front of her blouse already well saturated she thought the hell with it, and dove in without ceremony. When she caught one old man staring at her with a look of wonder in his eyes she winked at him and he reached over and patted her hand, laughing. It just might be all right, Liz thought — a little sticky at first but maybe it won't be so bad. She couldn't remember feeling so much at ease since before Glenn had asked her if she would mind living in Pakistan for a year. At that time her reaction had been decidedly negative. So help me, she had thought with deep resentment, he would commit his wife and daughter to live in purgatory for one of his projects.

She looked around at the open, friendly faces surrounding her in the hut. It sure isn't like home but there's not a cannibal in the lot, she thought, and reached over and patted the old man's hand in return. Pineapple juice streamed down his chin into the folds of white cloth he had wrapped around one shoulder. The old man poked the still older man sitting next to him and everybody laughed.

No business was discussed at the first meeting. One big worry was removed from Liz's mind when they were told that there was a hunting lodge on the edge of the village. It had been built by the Indian government before Partition to house visiting royalty who came to hunt in the forests that ringed the village. Liz pictured herself sleeping in a maharaja's bed and liked the idea. Of course, she thought, it's a long way to come for the experience but it just might be worth it, as long as I don't have to share it with a lot of snakes and spiders. Liz's younger brother had been bitten by a rattlesnake and had nearly died. The vivid memory of that event, which she had witnessed, had never left her, and she had grown up with a terrible dread of snakes and all potentially venomous creatures.

Pamela was totally absorbed and had very little to say. She was intimidated by the venerable age of their hosts. The whole setting was so totally different from anything she had imagined that it took some time for her to realize that this was actually it, that this was home for a year. In Wichita her fifth-grade class had given her a surprise party; the room was hung with posters her classmates had drawn representing their versions of her coming adventure. She had been a little put off by the many strange figures they had pictured surrounding her. They had had heavily painted faces. She hadn't thought of her coming trip in quite that light before and had been vaguely bothered by it ever since. As she looked around the room now she noted with great relief that there were no painted faces at all. Somehow that made it better.

Because Pamela sat lower on her chair than either

of her parents and could look out under the low-hanging thatch onto the flat plaza, she knew before they did that a crowd of people had gathered to await their reappearance. A good many children were in the group, a number of them, she was glad to see, of her own age. She noticed one boy about ten working his way along a fence that bordered the plaza. She felt there was something strange about him, but he was soon lost behind a group of adults and she turned to other thoughts. She would think about him later, but for the moment there was much too much to look at to linger long on any one impression.

When the meal of fruit, hard-boiled eggs, and tea was over, the Barclays were ushered out into the courtyard by the seven old men. Even Pamela was surprised at the size of the crowd that had gathered and stayed close to her father when they made their way through the throng. With quiet courtesy, the people opened a path for them. While Glenn was led to the side to greet two monks who taught in the school, Liz stopped to admire a couple of infants carried by mothers who didn't look much older than Pamela. One little girl brought a bunch of scarlet flowers forward and shyly presented them to her. Liz knelt to kiss the girl on the forehead, and the child quickly ran off between the legs of the adults and was not seen again.

A dozen or so of the villagers followed them as they were led out of the plaza to the path that ran back through the first valley. They crossed a small wooden bridge that spanned a deep, dry stream bed and then they went out through a set of gates. Once beyond the gates the path branched, trailing across dikes in the rice paddies in the valley below, and along the high ground that skirted the fields. Then each path branched out again.

Liz was pleasantly surprised by the sturdy hunting lodge. It was vast, having been designed during British rule to house twenty or thirty men and women on *shikar* after tiger, leopard, and wild elephant. The kitchen had a stone sink that had recently been scrubbed, and a hand pump promised fresh water from a deep well. The rooms were variously outfitted with beds, tables, and chairs, and one small room had a desk and even an ancient file cabinet. When they arrived their luggage had been stacked in neat piles in the center room and three young village men stood by, awaiting orders. As Liz moved to lift a suitcase off the pile, they sprang forward. She experienced for the first time the joys of having a staff of oriental houseboys. It would be a year before she would be able to lift her hand again in anything that resembled physical labor.

As her parents set about supervising the unpacking and the rearrangement of furniture in the half-dozen rooms they decided to use, Pamela asked permission to explore the village. Liz hesitated for a moment but couldn't find an answer to Glenn's "Why not?" and Pamela was permitted to go after promising not to approach the forest beyond the village proper.

Years later, when Pamela would try to reconstruct her first impressions of Pukmaranpur, she would be unable to do so. There was too much that was too different from anything she had ever known. It was a completely alien world. Neither the trees, the dress of the people, the shape of the buildings, nor the activities she witnessed as she wandered down path after path had any relationship to anything she had ever seen or even heard about. She was no longer a privileged and protected foreigner in a big car nudging its way through Karachi, Dacca or Chittagong. She was alone and on foot, a very conspicuous pale-faced little girl in a pink and white jumper and open-toed sandals.

At one point she came upon a group of girls about her own age. They were walking along the trail toward her, each carrying a load of fruit in a small, shallow basket set on her head. They stepped aside to let her pass without saying a word, but she heard them giggling once she was beyond them, and felt terribly lonely. She wanted to turn around and at least smile at them but couldn't find the nerve to do it. After all, she reflected, I'm new in the neighborhood. They should try to make me feel at home!

Somehow she managed to work her way around the central village and end up back in the plaza near the river. On the far side of the plaza the Buddhist school rose in repeated diminishing tiers of rough, dark wood rimmed with scalloped patterns cut out of tin. She could hear the school long before she saw it. The boys sitting on wicker mats inside, twenty feet above the plaza, were chanting a single phrase over and over again. She was fascinated by the sound and walked around the building until she stood underneath a balcony from which hung rows of recently laundered yellow robes. Moving out from under the balcony, she looked up directly into the face of a very old monk who was peering at her through a barred window. He wore thick glasses and his head was completely shaved. There was no discernible expression on his face and he looked out from behind the wooden bars like some kind of ominous caged animal.

Although the monk had been watching Pamela when she first passed the side of the school into the plaza and had seen her walk around the building to reappear under his window, she had not seen him. There was something frightening about his total lack of expression, and she ducked back under the balcony to get out of his line of vision. Once in the deep shadow she sought an escape route where the old man couldn't see her, and moved off, keeping very close to the building's foundations. As she rounded the corner she saw the boy again, the boy she had seen by the fence. Now she realized what was different about him. He was blind.

Pamela had inherited or at least absorbed her mother's sympathy for small injured creatures, human or otherwise. Instinctively she was drawn to the boy, as her mother would have been, and walked toward him. She was longing to talk to someone and the blind boy, at least, didn't seem threatening in any way.

Whether or not the boy had heard her approach she couldn't tell. When she was just a few feet away from where he was feeling his way along the fence she greeted him with as nonchalant a hello as she could manage.

The boy stopped and turned toward her.

"*Tumi ke?*"

Pamela knew it was a question and, reasonably assuming that he had asked her who she was, she answered with her name, which she repeated a second time slowly.

"*Nam?*"

Nam sounded enough like *name* to make sense to her and she repeated her name again. This time the boy repeated it, doing a fair job with the unfamiliar syllables.

"Yes, Pamela," she said.

Remembering what the boy had said to her when she first spoke she took the situation in hand and repeated it with a rising inflection.

"Tumi ke?"

"Khoka," the boy answered without hesitation and smiled.

Pamela stared at the boy. She was taken with the incredible change that came over his face when he smiled. In repose his face had a kind of dark, solemn beauty to it. Yet when he smiled it changed completely. He literally lit up, even though his eyes stared straight ahead and never moved to follow a sound.

"Apnar bari kothay?"

Pamela could not know the boy was asking her where her home was and was at a loss to answer what was obviously another question. She resorted to his name and said slowly, with a rising inflection, *"Nam Khoka?"*

"Hae, Khoka," he answered and then repeated "Paamela," meticulously separating each syllable.

In the distance she could hear a familiar voice also pronouncing her name and wondered how she was to take her leave of the boy. Instinctively she reached out and touched his arm.

"Goodbye, Khoka, I hope I see you again." She turned and ran up the path toward her mother's voice.

Khoka stood for a moment and then reached up with his left hand and pressed his fingers against the spot where her fingers had briefly rested. *"Adab,"* he said, *"Adab,* Paamela."

6

Early Days at Pukmaranpur

Glenn encountered his first major problem on his third day at Pukmaranpur. The dealer arrived by boat shortly after dawn to discuss the sale of two working elephants. Knowing the value of the American dollar, Glenn had anticipated a reasonable price for cows and tuskless males. When he was quoted twenty-four thousand rupees each, he saw his plans collapse. Ata, who was acting as interpreter, looked on with sympathy. "He might have warned me," Glenn thought petulantly, "he might have warned me."

"Twenty-four thousand rupees," he later complained to Liz, "that's over five thousand bucks each! A man works a full month here and gets thirty bucks. How in the hell do they figure an elephant for five thousand?"

He met with the merchant again the next day. Even though he explained through Ata that he didn't need a tusker for the work he planned, and that if his experiments went well elephant dealers would have a whole new market to sell to, the price stood. For a *makhna* or for a cow, the price was more than one hundred and sixty times the salary a laboring man could earn in a month.

The fact that his budget did not allow for the purchase of even one elephant was no minor setback for Glenn: it was the destruction of the very foundation of his experiment. Unless he could solve this one he might as well pack up and go back to Kansas, he lamented to Liz over a late-night cup of tea. He didn't really believe this, but it helped him to say it and then to have Liz tell him of her faith in his ability to solve the problem.

He recalled with mounting frustration the stories of India in the old days, days when princes and merchant-kings maintained private stables of twenty and more elephants. Then there were elephants to spare, elephants that did little more than carry bridegrooms to their weddings and royalty on tiger hunts. But he had to face it, those days had long since been consigned to the history books. Pakistan was no longer India, Maharajas were too busy being ambassadors and parliamentarians to take pride in enormous private stables, and the English had packed up and gone home. There was no one left who in civic-mindedness could loan him an elephant or two for at least a year. Elephants now belong to investors, and investors want a return on their rupees. To get someone to loan you an elephant would be like asking a contractor to loan you his bulldozer.

When all arguments with the elephant merchant had failed and when Manik and Masu, the two village elders who spoke English, failed to offer a reasonable alternative, Glenn turned to Ata.

"We'll have to catch our own elephants, Ata. What's involved?"

Ata explained the strict prohibition against catching wild elephants or disturbing wild herds without government permission and Glenn had visions of mountains of bureaucratic red tape piling up around them. It wasn't that bad, Ata explained, but it would require a trip back to Chittagong to confront the District Commissioner in his lair. He could issue the permits if he was sold on the necessity of the venture.

Glenn's knowledge of catching elephants was limited to what he had learned from the books he had read as a boy. He remembered two methods: the brutal pit technique of South India, a hangover from caveman days, and the stockade technique. To fill the great stockades wild herds were driven by scores of men on foot beating through the forest in the middle of the night, brandishing torches and throwing firecrackers. He knew without asking that his budget would not allow for the building of a stockade or for the hundreds of laborers and drivers who would ultimately be involved.

That problem, at least, became academic when Ata explained that the *khedda* or elephant drive was permitted only in the vicinity of Cox's Bazaar, and only in the month of December. The prospect of traveling two hundred miles to the south, establishing a one-time *khedda* operation there, and then waiting several months before making a catch was hopelessly unrealistic. Then, too, they would face the staggering task of transporting two or three green, and therefore very wild and dangerous, elephants across the lake and up the river. He doubted that a barge heavy enough for the job could even negotiate the waterways he had seen on his trip in.

Glenn sat looking helplessly at Ata. If I can't afford to buy or rent elephants, he thought, and I can't rig a drive, how do I experiment? The pit method was out. It was far too dangerous for the animals. Even if the District Commissioner would issue a permit, Glenn was unwilling to risk killing several wild elephants in order to get two to survive and pull his plows.

"There is one alternative, Glenn, *Mela shikar*."

"*Mela shikar?* I don't know what that is."

Ata went on to explain that in parts of Assam, Burma, and Nepal, and occasionally in the Chittagong Hill Tracts, there was a third method of catching wild elephants. They were noosed from the backs of *koonkis* by specially trained men. It was the most difficult and dangerous method for the men but was relatively safe for the prospective captives and required the minimum investment on the part of the initiators.

"You mean they actually lasso these monsters like cows? Is that possible?"

"Oh, it's quite possible. Bolo Bahadur that you saw at the river was a *mela shikar koonki* in the old days and Satwyne was a very famous *phandi*. They call the man who throws and manipulates the great noose the *phandi*."

Ata made some inquiries and came back with an estimate. If he could get the District Commissioner to issue a *mela shikar* permit for two elephants and if they could locate, capture, and break two animals in six weeks, the cost would be a little over five hundred dollars, and this included bringing a second *koonki* team of three men with their elephant in from another area over a hundred miles

61

away. There was no choice, as far as Glenn could see. Elephants cost over five thousand dollars apiece to buy, and only five hundred dollars a pair to capture — if he could get a permit, and if no one got killed in the process. He had once watched wild mustangs being roped in Nevada and had seen a man crippled trying to bring an eight-hundred-pound stallion under control. He found himself projecting that still vivid memory onto a roping operation involving an equally frightened and furious elephant weighing considerably over eight thousand pounds. The less he thought about it the better he felt.

It was while her husband was trying to sort out his king-sized elephant problem that Liz first began to realize that something was wrong, or about to go wrong. Both she and Glenn had been on a regular prophylactic course of chloroquin and Pamela had been on atabrine. Both drugs were specifics against malaria. They felt reasonably secure from other serious diseases because all of them had taken numerous shots before leaving the States. But Liz had reason to believe that things were not quite right. Suddenly without warning she would get a knifelike stabbing pain above her eyes, and this quickly built to a throbbing headache of almost blinding intensity. An hour or two in bed with three aspirin would alleviate most of the head pain, but she would awake feeling nauseated and listless and would lose her appetite entirely for twenty-four hours. The symptoms increased in severity and frequency throughout the period of the negotiations with the dealer and during the conferences with Ata about plans to launch a *mela shikar* operation.

When Glenn returned home with the news that he was going back down to Chittagong, he found Liz in bed, groaning with a temperature of a hundred and four point six. Her skin was parched and drawn and her eyes were glazed although she was still conscious. Frantically he called to Raanaa, the head houseboy, to bring freshly drawn well water and clean towels, and he began the course of treatment Dr. Hantman in Wichita and later Dr. Hessing in New York had prescribed for undiagnosed tropical fevers. As he stood over Liz bathing her with the damp, cold towels he whispered, "I did this to you, honey, didn't I?"

Exhausted by the fever and the pain, and because she hadn't eaten a reasonable meal in three days, Liz drifted off to sleep. She had a vague, free-floating feeling of regret as she heard herself say, somewhere far off, somewhere in the limbo of wracking fever, "Yes, you did."

It was forty-six hours after the onset of the fever before Liz awoke free of temperature and the shattering head pains. She felt neither hot nor cold, just tired and disconnected. She turned over and saw Glenn sleeping no more than three feet away.

Slowly her mind cleared and she began to fit the bits and pieces together. She could remember a few quick visits by Pamela, Glenn's constant attention and the pleasure she had felt, even at the worst of it, from the compresses and massage. She could remember his fingers rubbing her temples and the cold cloth pressed to her breasts. She could remember feeling vaguely uncomfortable about Raanaa moving around the room with fresh buckets of water as she lay there partially exposed, and she remembered, too, that she had been too sick and too tired to do anything but think vaguely about it.

She lay there for several minutes watching Glenn sleeping, breathing steadily and quietly. She had always loved the fact that he didn't snore; somehow snoring seemed vulgar to her and she appreciated this refinement in her husband. Then it suddenly occurred to her that he might be sick, too. She sat up, quickly recharged by the Earth-Mother instinct, but sank back again. She was dizzy and weak and a wave of nausea swept over her. Slowly she reconstructed her determination and forced herself up, rising first to her elbows, and then carefully the rest of the way. Inch by inch she swung her legs over the side of the bed and felt the harshness of the raw wooden floor beneath her bare feet. With great care she stood, wavered slightly but managed to remain erect. She inched over to her husband's bed and sat down heavily beside him. He turned and moaned and opened his eyes as she placed her hand on his forehead and found to her great relief that he wasn't feverish. He looked up at her and smiled, then he remembered.

"What the hell are you doing out of bed?"

"Just checking up on you."

"On me! What about you? How do you feel, honey?"

"Like I just pipped my egg. Well drained and all used up. How are you doing?"

He was sitting on the bed beside her with his arm around her shoulders.

"You know, Mrs. B., you scared hell out of me. You really did."

"Well, it was your idea to come to this damn place, not mine."

"It really is my fault, isn't it? That's all I've been thinking about since you took sick. I even had nightmares about it."

"No, Glenn, don't. It's not your fault, it's not anyone's. You're a man and you have to follow your career. I'm a woman and I have to follow my man. That's the way things are put together in this world so why fight it? I'm sorry I was such a bitch about coming here and about all the fuss I've made. I'll be better, I promise."

Glenn gently pulled her closer and she let her head loll against his chest. He ran his free hand up under her throat and cradled her chin in his palm.

"We'll make it, Liz. We always have, and before you know it you'll be packing to go home."

"I know we will, Glenn, I know it. But I'll tell you one thing, they have bugs here the likes of which I never met in Wichita!"

The first few days after Pamela had encountered Khoka near the Buddhist school had been busy ones for her parents. Glenn had been totally engrossed in the overriding problem of obtaining elephants for the experiment and Liz had been involved in establishing a home. Then Liz's fever had started and Pamela was forced to keep her distance except for a few hurried visits allowed more to reassure her that her mother was alive than anything else. Her care was left almost exclusively to Raanaa, who was proving to be invaluable.

Fortunately, Pamela had other matters on her mind. She had adopted Khoka. He didn't know it yet but she had made up her mind to help him. She wasn't quite sure what that meant but she had taken him on just as she might a stray kitten or a bird that had fallen from its nest. She talked of little else at home and as Liz and Glenn began to recover from the anxiety of Liz's illness, Pamela's endless talk of the little blind boy in the village started to register. They complimented her on her concern for a less fortunate person but cautioned her against moving too precipitously into a situation none of them really knew anything about. But Pamela was like Liz, which meant that Khoka had a benefactor, like it or not.

In fact, Pamela and Khoka had a going friendship of sorts although they were still unable to communicate on anything but the most primitive level. Without being able to resort to gestures Pamela was stymied much of the time. They met every day and greeted each other in proper Bengali fashion. Pamela had learned that *adab* means "hello," "goodbye," or any other salutation that is appropriate to the moment. Then they would sit together trying desperately to communicate. It wasn't working very well so far, but Pamela was determined. First she would learn Bengali, and teach Khoka English at the same time, then she would learn all about him, and *then* she would decide how to help him.

The blue and white launch that was scheduled to appear once a week wasn't due for another two days. Its arrival would mark Glenn's departure for Chittagong and his visit to the District Commissioner. He was sitting and sipping streaming tea with Manik in the long, low building on the edge of the village plaza, when he saw a slender young boy moving along the fence near the Buddhist school, obviously feeling his way as he went. He assumed it was Khoka from Pamela's description of him. He was quite dark, with a shock of extremely shiny black hair.

"Manik, you have a blind boy in the village. Who is he?"

"*Hae*. Khoka. The unlucky one."

"What happened? Has he always been blind?"

Manik shook his head sadly and looked down as he explained. Khoka, to Glenn's surprise, was the son of Satwyne, the *phandi*. He had been born a normal child and was a joy to his father and to his doting mother, Riboy. Riboy had been a beautiful girl who adored her child. She called him Khoka-*moni*, "Khoka, my jewel."

There had been the promise of bad luck from the very beginning. A tramp had wandered into the village on the day Khoka was born and had gotten very drunk on some palm wine that he carried in an earthenware jug. He was sleeping on the ground not far from Satwyne's hut at the time of Khoka's birth. Some children had come running by and one boy stumbled over him. He rose up in his drunken stupor and screamed after the children. Just as the midwife handed Khoka to Riboy for the first time she heard a strange, coarse voice scream, *"Jahan-namey ja bitla kothakar"* ("Go to hell, you little brat"). Riboy thought the curse was being leveled at her son, then only seconds old. She wept in terror and asked for special prayers to offset the curse. Satwyne in a fit of anger went out and knocked the man to the ground and then ran him out of the village. He was found dead in the forest a few days later. To Riboy it had all been a bad omen and it came back to haunt her on nights when she had difficulty sleeping.

Khoka's growth was normal, however, and his early childhood both healthy and happy. But one morning shortly after Khoka had turned four, Riboy arose at dawn and walked out of the house. The first bird she heard from the edge of the forest was the cursed *pappia*. No one could tell you what a *pappia* looked like, Manik assured Glenn, because no one would look at one. The cry of the *pappia* sounds in the Bengali language like "Oh, my eyes are gone." It is the very worst of luck to hear a *pappia* at the beginning of a day before hearing any other bird.

To make matters worse, just as the sun reached its zenith on that day, a strange yellow *kookoor* (dog) appeared outside of Satwyne's hut and began howling for no apparent reason. A *kookoor* howling at noon is an omen almost as evil as the *pappia's* call at daybreak. The yellow dog had never been seen in the village before and was never seen again.

Riboy was uneasy for the rest of the day and kept Khoka very close to her. Whether it was because his mother communicated her tension to him, or because she wouldn't let him play in the plaza in front of the house, Khoka was cranky and fussed through most of the afternoon. It was with great relief that Riboy finally sang him to sleep and was able to relax for the first time since daybreak. Her premonitions of tragedy began to ease.

Later that night a terrible storm moved into the valley. Rain slashed across the village and many homes were damaged. The wind screamed in the trees and dogs whimpered as they huddled under the huts. Babies were heard crying and men rushed about trying to secure their belongings against the wind. Shortly after the wind and rain began there were fires in the sky. Thunder rolled in with such violence that not a person in the village could sleep. Then lightning struck. A huge banyan tree near the school split down the middle. Half of it fell onto a group of three huts and men ran from all directions to help. Just as Satwyne ran out of his hut, with the terrified Riboy screaming after him not to go, lightning struck again. This time it was his own home. The explosive bolt was so powerful that Satwyne, who was a dozen feet away, was hurled to the ground. When he stumbled to his feet his house had all but vanished. Only a smoldering pile of rubble was left. His beloved Riboy was dead, burned almost beyond recognition, and Khoka was wandering around with his hands stretched out before him, calling for his mother. He was blind. In a matter of months he lost all memory of vision. Nor did he seem to remember anything about the terrible night when his mother died.

Glenn listened carefully, studying the face of the old man as he spoke. The quiet, even good sense of the elder and his careful choice of words seemed to run counter to his obvious belief in evil omens. It was a contradiction Glenn found difficult to fathom.

"Manik, do you believe that the curses of a drunken tramp, the call of a bird and the howling of a dog caused the boy's blindness? Do you really believe that yourself?"

"Some things in this world cause other things to happen, others only foretell them. It is difficult to know one from the other. When I was young I hoped that age would bring me that kind of wisdom. Age has disappointed me."

The old man studied his visitor for a long time. He looked deeply into his eyes, then looked him up and down. Glenn found himself staring back. When Manik spoke again his words came very softly.

"Are you a Christian?"

"Of a sort, yes. Not a very impressive one, but a Christian."

"Then you believe that a child was born of a woman who had never been had by a man. You *know* this to be true. You cannot repeat that incident, you cannot explain it or really understand it. Why, then, must I explain to you that which I know to be true but which I cannot really understand?"

Glenn thought of all of the buildings he had been in, new buildings in big American cities, that lacked a thirteenth floor. Then he remembered Liz's pleading insistence that none of their coming child's clothing or furniture be bought before the birth — and how he had had to run around for two days after Pamela arrived checking purchases off the long list Liz had given to him before she had gone into the hospital. He felt trapped because he could not bring himself to admit to the old man that he was right, right at least in accepting the fact that there is an unknown world of cause and effect. He knew that Khoka's blindness was the result of some rational cause, not the product of a drunken curse, the call of a bird, or the howling of a dog. But what he didn't know, he was forced to admit, was whether these things had actually foretold the tragedy.

"Has the boy ever been examined by a doctor?"

Manik told him about the visit of a doctor to the village several years earlier, and the coming of a nurse several times after that. The boy had been examined as a matter of course but all they could tell Satwyne was what he already knew. Khoka was blind and probably always would be.

That night Glenn recounted the conversation to

Liz and Pamela. They listened intently and after he had finished Pamela went to her room to think. Liz looked at her husband for a moment and then suggested, "There's a hospital in Chittagong. Take Khoka down the river with you. It will probably be the only chance he'll ever have in his whole life. Take him with you, and take Pamela along to look after him. If you don't owe it to Khoka, you owe it to her."

Glenn tried to get Liz to go on the trip as well, but she argued that although her illness had obviously run its course, the journey could only make her more tired than she already was. She continued to press the case for Khoka, and Glenn couldn't think of a single reasonable argument in rebuttal. And so it was decided. After dinner Glenn again sought out Manik, who took him to Satwyne. The *phandi* sat listening while Manik explained the plan. He walked to the door where he stood for several minutes with his back to the room and then turned back, nodding his assent.

By the time Glenn got back to the lodge Pamela was asleep. He and Liz strolled onto the veranda and looked out over the paddies. A full moon lit the orderly blocks of cultivated land in a pale silvery light and beyond them the forest stood in black silhouette against the sky.

"Well, do you feel more at home now that you've got somebody else to worry about?"

"And you? I suppose you don't care about the boy."

"I care, darling, I care."

"We call that *bhalobasa*, Glenn."

"O.K., so what's *bhalobasa*?"

"It's the first word in any language. *Bhalobasa* in Bengali means 'love.' "

7

The District Commissioner
and the Doctor

The trip back down the Gamalbuk to Lake Karnaphuli was uneventful except that it gave Glenn a
second opportunity to examine the jungle along the
upper river and the swamp in the lower reaches.
He was a great deal more aware of the birdlife than
he had been on the trip in and caught fleeting
glimpses of an enormous rusty-brown wild boar
and some swamp deer on one of the riverine islands.

Although it was impossible for him to convey his
feelings, for Khoka the trip was bewilderingly ex-

citing. He had come to feel comfortable in Pamela's presence. Although he had had some misgivings when Satwyne explained to him what was about to happen, he thought of Pamela's soft voice and the reassuring way she had of reaching out and touching his hand or arm. The thought of being with her for an uninterrupted period of time delighted him and he accepted the idea without condition or appeal. Not since Riboy's death had anyone given him so much attention. He had learned to live without that kind of softness because he had to. But he had never ceased needing it.

For most of the trip downriver he and Pamela sat cross-legged on the deck in front of a mountain of pineapples and continued their reciprocal language lessons. Although Pamela was too short on vocabulary and syntax to express her intent, Khoka understood the plan and entered into the game with as much enthusiasm as she did.

"Angul," Pamela repeated, pressing her finger against his, and he repeated slowly, "fin-gehr." His voice was soft and pleasant and had a faint musical quality to it. Since all of his communication with others was through the medium of voice alone he listened carefully and modulated his replies meticulously. *"Kan,"* she said, as he pronounced "ee-yehr." She managed *"cibuk"* well enough but he had difficulty with "chin" and it came out variously as "hchin" and "sin." There was a lot of giggling

and the frequent errors were taken as a matter of course. The further they got into it the more intent they became. While it was still essentially a recreation, they had a mutual longing to comprehend and instinctively they knew that this game was an indispensable prelude. They played it with an intensity that surprised Glenn as he sat off to the side watching them.

"Elbow" Khoka said; "*konui*," Pamela remembered accurately. "*Mukh*," he said. "Face," she responded. Pamela hesitated when Khoka took her hand and pressed her fingers against his eye. "*Cokh*," he said and waited. "*Cokh*," he said again. Finally she managed to say it, and he replied, "aye," without self-consciousness. Glenn turned away. It was a long time since he had felt the sting of tears but the expression on Pamela's face was more than he could take in stride. As he turned he could hear the game continuing: "*pa*," "foot"; "*cul*," "hair."

The District Commissioner was not at all what Glenn had expected. He was young — no more than twenty-eight, Glenn calculated — and dressed in expensive Western casual dress. His slacks were English, his low, highly polished jodhpur boots probably the same, and his tailored raw-silk sport shirt was fashioned after a safari coat, with four patch pockets and a matching belt. His English was impeccable, obviously the result of his having been educated abroad.

"I will issue your license for two elephants, Mr.

Barclay, but you must accept responsibility for the safety of all concerned. *Mela shikar* is not a sporting event. It is a very dangerous business and many died at it in the old days. My father once attended a *maiden shikar* before Partition and saw three deaths in one afternoon."

He was referring to the type of *mela shikar* that is carried out on an open, grassy plain. Glenn could envision the advantage wild elephants would have with uninterrupted visibility and maneuvering room.

He swallowed hard because he wasn't at all sure about what he was going to say. This is it, he thought, here and now, or no experiment.

"I am fully prepared to accept all responsibility, and I do appreciate the . . . ah, problems involved."

"Good. Yes, you shall have your license and my wishes for good luck. I would suggest, though, that you have your men avoid the tuskers. They are apt to want to take one for the prestige that comes to them, but they can be very dangerous. Remember, you are responsible for your men as well as the *koonkis* and they can be quite foolhardy at times."

Glenn realized that the Commissioner had been thinking of his responsibility for the elephants — while Glenn himself had been thinking of the men. My God! he thought. All I have to do is get a couple of *koonkis* skewered by a tusker and there goes the budget for the year!

The Commissioner rang for his secretary, who appeared in rather startling contrast to his employer. He was a middle-aged man with a long, flowing moustache and a shock of black hair. He was barefooted and wore a rather untidy cotton *lungi*, a loose-fitting wrap-around, with a bunch of keys hanging from a large safety pin. He nodded in reply to the Commissioner's rapidly issued instructions and returned a few minutes later with a form and a hand embossing machine. With exaggerated care, Glenn thought, the Commissioner set aside the pen and embossed a seal over his neat little signature. How incredible it is, Glenn reflected, how many of a man's dreams can depend on nothing more than another man's autograph.

Tea was served and Glenn had a chance to learn something he hadn't realized before. The Commissioner, who acknowledged that he was just twenty-five, was a very nice guy. He was a little disappointed that his visitor didn't share his enthusiasm for soccer and didn't know one team from another. He really surprised Glenn by discussing Australia's last go at the America's Cup. Before tea was over Glenn thoroughly liked him and voiced the hope that he would visit Pukmaranpur and see how the experiment was going. The Commissioner assured him he would. As they walked to the door he took a small carved box from a bookshelf and gave Glenn a bracelet made from what appeared to be thick plastic strands.

"I brought this from Kenya last year. It is made from the tail hairs of the African elephant. It is supposed to keep the wearer safe from wild animals. Perhaps our Asiatic elephants will accord recognition to their African cousins. Good luck."

That's got to be one of the nicest bureaucrats in the whole world, Glenn thought, as he walked across the lawn to where Pamela and Khoka sat under a tree waiting for him. Good lord, they're still at it, he said half aloud.

"Aek, dui, tin, car, pac, choy," Pamela said. "Run, two, tree, four, fivah, sex," Khoka pronounced with obvious pride in his accomplishment.

Dr. Noor listened without interrupting. He was as impeccably dressed and as fluent in English as the Commissioner had been. Somehow, though, his accent was different. Glenn couldn't resist asking him where he had gone to school.

"Harvard," the doctor said. "I did my internship at Queens General in New York and my residency at Beth Israel in Boston. I miss it. I loved the States but my obligation is here. It was very difficult coming back after nearly thirteen years. I still think of the States as my home."

"What do you miss most?"

"Honestly? Dating. It's a lovely custom. But this is a Moslem country and if I take a girl out she is automatically considered to be of ill repute. It's very difficult. My parents are trying to arrange a suitable marriage for me now. I just hope she is good-looking. I'm afraid the States spoiled me."

Glenn and the doctor walked out to where Pamela and Khoka were sitting on a wooden bench. They had found the hospital corridor intimidating and the constant flow of people too distracting. They sat side by side quietly, their game temporarily at an end.

"*Adab*, Khoka," the doctor said as he took the boy's hand. Glenn sat down beside Pamela and watched the doctor lead Khoka off down the hall.

After a few minutes the doctor came back alone and suggested that they return in three hours. The tests that were required would take that long and there was little point in their sitting on a hard bench in the underlit corridor.

After lunch in the sad little dining room of the Hotel Hawaii, Chittagong's one attempt at public hospitality, Pamela and Glenn walked near the docks amid the incredible surge of life that is the hallmark of every oriental port. It reminded Glenn of some kind of eternal bazaar, the kind he had read of in Halliburton, Sanderson and Kipling. People, crates, animals, piles of produce, and raw materials he couldn't identify were jammed together amid smells and sounds that seemed to drum at them as they walked along. Several small boys came running toward them asking for *bhikkha* and although Glenn knew better he passed around some coins of low denomination. The word spread rapidly and they finally had to retreat to the Microbus that had been hired for the day. They were openly pursued by flocks of children coming from all directions, each trying to outdo the others in the performance he put on. Some feigned a limp so badly that it was a comic rather than dramatic display, while others attempted to sound as if they were in pain or starving to death. The croaking voices and forced hoarse whispers coming from the lithe and generally healthy young bodies were silly enough to make Pamela want to laugh. She wasn't entirely sure, though, that her father was right and that the kids swarming around them wanted money for ice cream and not to take home to a starving household, so she kept her face as straight as she could. Before closing the Microbus door against the swarm, Glenn tossed a fistful of *paisas* onto a grassy plot and the kids piled up in a wild free-for-all. He marveled at how little hostility they showed in the mad scramble. Thank God, it's a game, he thought.

"There is nothing organically wrong with the boy's eyes, Mr. Barclay. His optic nerves are perfectly healthy and there is no sign that there has ever been any disease to cause blindness."

The doctor stood next to Khoka with his hand resting on the boy's shoulder. Pamela stood beside her father trying to translate the doctor's words into terms she could understand herself.

"Then why is he blind?"

"Do you know what a conversion-reaction is?"

"Not really. I've heard the expression, but I'd appreciate your explaining it to me."

The doctor explained that Khoka had stopped seeing because the last thing he had seen was too painful for him to bear. It was a form of hysteria, a turning inward of shock until it had become a physical manifestation. Khoka, unconsciously, didn't want to see because he was afraid of what painful experience his sight might bring him. Dr. Noor admitted that since he wasn't a psychiatrist, the diagnosis was really nothing more than a very reasonable guess on his part, but all signs pointed to its probability.

"Is there a cure?"

"Perhaps, but I can't tell you how to administer it. Khoka has to *want* to see again."

At the mention of his name Khoka turned his face up toward the doctor. The doctor looked down at him and squeezed the back of his neck gently.

"If there is ever something he wants to see badly enough, or if ever he undergoes a shock as great as the one he had that night, his sight could return as quickly as it vanished. It could even be a matter of faith. If he ever develops enough faith in his ability to see, it could happen that way, too. No one can say how or when it could happen. At least, it would take a man far wiser than a mere doctor."

Glenn looked at Khoka and admitted to himself for the first time that he wasn't doing this for Pamela at all. He desperately wanted the boy to see. He had an almost uncontrollable urge to take him and shake him and *demand* that he see, that he stop playing at being blind. He realized the foolishness of his reaction and realized, as well, that that kind of foolishness came only from deep concern.

"One other thing, Mr. Barclay. I would advise you against discussing this with the boy. Everything that has happened to him has occurred far out of reach of his conscious mind. He would gain nothing by hearing about it. It could only confuse and depress him. It's not something he can handle in any part of his mind that you can reach. It would take a very different kind of experience from any you could safely provide. One can never tell what another person's reaction to shock will be. It could restore his sight, or it could push him over a cliff. Khoka has been teetering on the edge of a cliff for a long time. His blindness could be the thread that keeps him from falling over. You see, he remembers very well what happened that night. It's all still with him, only he has it put away in a pocket where he can't reach it. In a way he's being merciful to himself. Take him home, Mr. Barclay. This is beyond your capabilities, and beyond mine. You don't have to feel guilty about it, I do. As a doctor I am *supposed* to be able to heal."

8

Preparations

Pamela wasn't sure when she first thought about it.
The idea just evolved and then she was thinking
about it to the exclusion of everything else. They
were halfway up the river and she stood back watching her father at the rail. He just has to agree, she
thought, he just has to! She watched him carefully,
trying to gauge his mood. She had enough feminine
instinct to know that timing can mean everything
when dealing with a man.

It was a running battle between her natural caution

and her enthusiasm. She was bursting with it, far too full of it, to contain it, and her caution lost.

"Daddy, I have an idea."

"What is it, honey?" Glenn turned around and leaned back against the rail, looking down into the earnest little face.

"You've got to promise to hear it all before you make up your mind. You can't say 'no' until you have thought about it. Okay?"

"Okay. I promise."

"Well now, Daddy . . . the doctor said that Khoka might not see again, at least for a long time, unless something happens, and we can't make that thing happen because we don't know what it is. Right?"

It seemed to Glenn that he loved his daughter more at these moments than at any others, when she was so very serious and about to launch into a lecture or an act of persuasion. He wanted to pick her up and tickle her and bite her ear as he used to, but out of deference to her feelings he played it straight.

"That's right."

"Then Daddy — now this is the idea and you promised not to say 'no' until you thought about it for a long time."

"That's right, I promised."

Pamela took a deep breath.

"Daddy, let's buy Khoka a Seeing Eye dog."

Glenn's first reaction was not exactly positive. A

Seeing Eye dog, he thought, where in hell would we get a Seeing Eye dog out here? But he held back, as he had promised. Then, as he looked down at his serious little daughter, his attitude began to change. It would be good for the boy, but there was more to it than that. The reaction on the part of the villagers would be good, but there was an even more important aspect yet. He was certain that no one in the village had ever heard of a dog being trained to lead the blind. Dogs, the mongrel dogs seen around native villages, were not held in very high repute. Potentially, his most difficult task in the months ahead would be to convince the people of Pukmaranpur that another familiar animal, the elephant, might be used in ways they had never dreamed of. His whole experiment depended on their quick acceptance of that idea. What better way to start things off, what more subtle way than this?

"Okay, honey, okay. It's a great idea."

Pamela couldn't believe it had been so easy. She was suddenly in her father's arms, kissing him, telling him how much she loved him.

Glenn gave the message to the launch captain, written out in big block capitals. He gave him enough money to cover the cost of the cable to his firm's office in Wichita and instructed him to dispatch it as soon as he returned to Kaptai. If he stopped at Rangamati on the way down, he was to send it from there. It was all that easy. Within half an hour

Pamela's idea had been born, matured, transmitted and put into action.

Exactly ninety-six hours later a telegram was received at the Barclay, Jamin & Norris office in Wichita confirming the order that had been made by long-distance telephone within an hour after Glenn's cable had been received. Orders for trained guide dogs are normally far in excess of available animals, but the special character of the request, coupled with the fact that an experienced dog had suddenly become available due to the death of its master, worked the miracle that was needed. In another ninety-six hours, eight days after Pamela had first had the idea, Prince was loaded into a crate and put aboard a plane in San Francisco. Five thousand one hundred and thirty-one air miles later he was fed, walked and watered in Tokyo. Three hours later he was taken for a short walk in Hong Kong, at the airport at Kowloon, and again in Bangkok, one thousand and sixty-five air miles closer to Pukmaranpur. He was fed again in New Delhi, and transferred to a 727 in Karachi for the flight back across the top of India to Dacca. In the zig-zag flight pattern he was the victim of the trouble between India and Pakistan. Few direct flights between the two countries are permitted.

There had been some small oversight in the paper work at Karachi, and Prince was kept, crated, for eleven hours in Dacca while a minor bureaucrat was routed out to put his initials on a slip of paper stapled to the import manifest. During that period no one thought to walk, water or feed the crated dog. Prince huddled in his own filth in a corner of the tin-roofed shack. It is doubtful that he would have survived many more hours. Two clouded leopards being shipped out to a zoo in Germany had perished in the same building only a few weeks before.

It was a badly frightened, very soiled and totally bewildered German shepherd that was finally loaded onto the blue and white launch at Kaptai for the trip across the lake and up the river to Pukmaranpur.

While Pamela had done little since their return to Pukmaranpur but count the hours, the hours of Prince's travail, her father had had other matters to think about. With the license in hand for the capture of two wild elephants, he had elaborate preparations to make. A runner was dispatched to Chimbuk, there to locate the owner of the *koonki* Sabal Kali, who in combination with Bolo Bahadur would effect the captures. It was a strange combination, Glenn would come to realize, for while Bolo Bahadur was a *makhna* or tuskless male, Sabal Kali was a *sakhni*, a female with tusks. Sabal Kali's owner or *koonkidar* was also the *phandi* who would work with Satwyne in the forests behind Pukmaranpur.

In the surprisingly short time of two weeks the runner was back with the message that the *koonkidar* Oroon was getting ready to leave with his two-man team and would be in the vicinity of Pukmaranpur in less than two weeks. That would be just enough time, Ata assured Glenn, to get things ready for their operation.

Satwyne had to work his old team up into good form. They had been tilling the soil for years, and the extraordinarily sharp reflexes needed by a *phandi* team that expected to survive a capture were dangerously dulled. It reminded Glenn of an old Western he had once seen where a gunfighter dug out his gear after years of retirement and practiced fast draws in order to right a new wrong. Satwyne, Ma, his second in command, and Kala, the third member, went to an unused field outside the agricultural area to practice maneuvers and noose throws. They concentrated on Bolo Bahadur's footwork and response to commands.

A relay team of observers went off to the forest each morning to bring back news of the wild elephants in the area. To make their captures within the stipulated period of time, to make them as close to the village as possible, and to get exactly the animals they wanted, they needed to know what elephants were in the area and what their movements were likely to be at the beginning of the *shikar* operation. A chart began to grow in the hunting lodge showing movements and assigning names to the wild animals that the teams reported.

There was a *mal jooria* reported from an area

north of the village. This small group of bulls might be able to provide them with candidates for their plows, but there was an air of uncertainty about the group. Its size varied from two to three bulls, changing a couple of times a week. Masu shook his head when he was shown the record of the count and advised against it. The fact that the group seemed unable to hold together for more than a couple of days at a time suggested that a bad-acting *goonda* or rowdy might be associated with it. Elephant society, like its human counterpart, has its outlaws. No honest man or beast has ever profited from an association with them. The members of the group were assigned the names of Mutt, Jeff and Mr. X. As a group they were referred to as the Mafia.

There were two *mreegas* traveling with a group of five cows to the west of the village. The *mreega* is a weedy or scrawny deer-like elephant that can make a good worker within limits but is prone to weakness. Three of the cows had calves and the other two were apparently *sarins*, young cows that had not yet calved. The group was known as Able, Baker and the Rockettes.

Hour by hour, day by day, Glenn's store of elephant lore grew. He found it increasingly fascinating and asked endless questions of Ata, Manik, and Masu, and through them of Satwyne. Two thousand years of working with a species of animal can build up more than a special vocabulary. He wanted to learn it all. Ata was intrigued by his enthusiasm for the project and admitted to himself, and then to Glenn, that he now knew why Glenn had been selected for the tricky assignment. He was not a horse and cow man, but an animal man. He instinctively understood problems as they arose, and got on with the experienced elephant men as if he had been among them for years.

The most promising reports came from an area a dozen miles south of the village. A small mixed herd seemed to be established in the region, using regular trails and bathing sites. The runners reported that the herd consisted of twelve animals, two among them apparently *koomeriahs*. The *koomeriah* is the show animal of the elephant world. It is the royal breed, the most expensive animal to buy, the one that brings the most prestige to the owner, and, quite naturally, the hardest to find. The breed is characterized by short, solid hind legs and a massive body. The skin is tough and heavily wrinkled, the head is large and noble and the trunk is heavy and thick. Either a *makhna* or cow of this caste is just a notch below a male *koomeriah* or royal tusker, but for the agricultural program they would be better than good. It was possible, Masu cautioned, that the two animals weren't as good as the runners were reporting. They were probably *dwasalas*, animals midway between the prized *koomeriah* and the very much less desirable *mreegas*. Right now, Glenn thought, I'd take a billy goat if he had a trunk. But the two-thousand-year-old traditions and enthusiasms of the elephant men were not to be denied. Glenn lay awake at night thinking of his two *koomeriahs*, who became bigger and bigger and more and more wrinkled as the nights wore on. "Do you know," he confided to Liz, "I'm really hooked by this business. These bloody walking mountains get under your skin!"

It was decided to establish the *pilkhana* — *the* training depot — south of the village. It is difficult and dangerous work for *koonkis* to transport newly captured animals over great distances. They are badly frightened, and often struggle fiercely. It sometimes takes brute strength on the part of the *koonkis* to hold them in check and it is exhausting work. Newly captured animals often struggle so hard that they either kill themselves or are injured so badly that they have to be destroyed. The shorter the distance that the struggling captives have to be dragged between two *koonkis* the better their chances of survival. Establishing the *pilkhana* south of the village, then, was a calculated gamble on the stability of the small herd with the questionable *koomeriahs* in that area. The herd was code-named "Likely."

Pamela's day finally arrived. Raanaa brought the news of the launch's arrival and Pamela darted through the village, heading for the river. As she arrived, the launch owner's son was leading Prince ashore on a short lead. Pamela ran up to the dog and knelt on the ground before him. She looked into his face and took the tag that hung from his collar. "Prince," she read aloud. "I love you, Prince." The dog pushed his nose against her, sniffed under her chin, and licked her face. As she took him by the lead and set off in search of Khoka she was crying with happiness. Liz and Glenn remained off to the side, allowing Pamela to savor her long, agonizingly anticipated moment of joy.

9

Mela Shikar

For generations the special qualities that constituted Prince's nature, intelligence, and appearance had been carefully nurtured, enhanced, and guided. In Germany, in the early days of his breed, specimens with less than an acceptable potential were put to death lest their weaknesses be carried forward and inadvertently reintroduced into the line. Derived from old breeds of farm and herding dogs and fostered as the *Deutsche Schäferhinde* since the formation of the first club in Germany in 1899, his kind had patrolled with soldiers, walked the greasy lanes of darkened factories, escorted police, guarded homes and children, and finally led the blind. He was a working dog with a working dog's reliable temperament, almost unlimited patience and incredible power to resist temptation. Lesser dogs could yap and snarl, cats could hiss and spit, and strangers could beckon and tempt, but Prince, once set on a task, was immovable. He was a special dog from a special breed, the combination of man's determination and nature's endless capacity for variations on a theme. He was a creature of both, by both created and of each a servant.

A person deprived of a sense, whether child or adult, seeks a more intense relationship with his environment through those avenues that remain intact. Blind people hear better and have a finer sense of touch than most sighted people. Khoka was no exception. Although he had never been introduced to the miracle of Braille he read the world around him with his fingers. They never ceased their explorations and once they came upon a new object his curiosity was boundless until he knew all that his fingers could tell him. You cannot glance with your fingers, for they have no peripheral vision. Examination by touch is examination in depth.

Khoka knelt and ran his hands over Prince's head. The shepherd stood square and patient, allowing the boy to feel the corners of his mouth and then run his fingers over his muzzle. Across the ridges arching above his eyes Khoka's inquiring fingers moved. They followed the curve of his crown to where his alert ears stood expectantly erect. This kind of touch introduction is the first thing a Seeing Eye dog must expect when meeting a new master. Khoka's hands felt across the dog's great paddle-broad shoulders, explored the point where his elbows lay in against his ribs and ran down the straight, firm forelegs. Finally Prince stirred, bent his cold black nose to Khoka's cheeks and pressed against him. Khoka threw his arms around the dog's solid muscular neck and buried his face. Every child loves and needs the touch and the security of a warm body of fur. How much more so a child of eternal night.

"Baba. Bhalobasi tahake."

Pamela understood his simple pronouncement of love for the dog. She felt, not without considerable justification, that this was the most important thing she had ever done. She felt as well that she was no longer an observer of a real-life situation, but a part of it. Her not yet eleven-year-old body may not have been up to it, but her soul was, and she was having her first real go at motherhood. She was, after all, her mother's daughter.

They were sitting in front of Satwyne's hut: Satwyne, Pamela and Khoka. Some neighbors stood off to one side watching, curious about the fuss being made over the strange-looking but admittedly handsome dog. It had been rumored for over two weeks that a special kind of *Kookoor* was coming to Khoka, a gift of the foreigners, but it wasn't clear what this special quality was to be or how it would manifest itself. They watched, not commenting, patiently waiting to see what would happen now that the special dog had arrived.

Prince couldn't do anything miraculous, of course, nothing that would leave them gaping in wonder. The miracle of his skill would reveal itself gradually in the days that followed. It would be a combination of his own skill and Khoka's faith in him.

Later that same day Glenn arrived with Ata and explained the dog's talents to Satwyne and Khoka. He had read and reread the letter of instructions that had come with Prince. He felt a special responsibility in the matter since the organization that supplied Prince had waived the normal training period required for dog and owner to work together. Khoka had to learn to speak the basic commands in English and learn the correct responses to Prince's actions. He proved to be a good student.

In the days that followed the people of Pukmaranpur came to understand the *kookoor's* special qualities and stopped to watch as Khoka walked across open areas and along the river bank, places where he had never dared go before. Khoka no longer had to feel his way along fences or huddle in lonely fear close to the foundations of the buildings around the plaza. With Prince leading the way he found a world that had been locked away from him.

Before his first week in Pukmaranpur was up, Prince was able to demonstrate the full measure of his talents. It was an event that caused endless talk in the huts that night. Khoka and Prince were walking along the high bank overlooking the river. A tree root stuck up out of the ground for about a foot, creating a hazard in the form of a low, woody arch. Prince sidestepped the obstruction as his training had taught him to do and tried to move Khoka around it by using his hip against the boy's legs. Khoka misunderstood and moved straight ahead. His foot caught in the root and he lost his balance, letting go of Prince's harness. He barely hit the water before Prince plunged in only inches away. As soon as Khoka surfaced Prince had him by his shirt and dragged him up onto the bank. At least a dozen people saw what had happened. Dog and boy were led back to Satwyne's hut and a great deal was said about the strange dog that could be eyes to a person without them, and protector of a child from all harm.

Ten days later, when Prince lunged and threw Khoka aside as a cobra reared up in the grass beside a pathway, the villagers marveled again. It was decided that the stranger who wanted the elephants was a magician who could instill in animals qualities they had had before only in legends. When Ata brought the news of what the people were saying, Glenn smiled. I hope they don't carry that idea too far, he thought. I may disappoint them very badly.

The *koonkidar* Oroon arrived with his powerful Sabal Kali and runners were dispatched to the forest south of the village for a final survey. Every move the wild herd made was to be reported. If the elephants appeared to be drifting away from the village the *koonki* teams would have to move out immediately. It was hoped, however, that the herd would swing around, as it had done about every fifth day in the weeks past, and come closer to the proposed catching and training area. Glenn was still concerned about the miles of heavily wooded country that lay between the village and the herd. He wanted to take his prizes as close in as possible.

While the two *phandis* moved their *koonkis* into a holding area four miles south of the village Glenn stood by his command post in the hunting lodge. Runners arrived almost hourly and the herd's movements were carefully plotted on a map that had been drawn with the help of Manik and Masu. Glenn bided his time. He would in all probability have only one go at the herd and a wrong move could be disastrous. The naturally cautious animals could scatter or become so alerted to impending danger before the operation even began that it would become impossible to move in on them undetected.

Pamela, in the meantime, was spending more and more time with Khoka. The first few days after Prince arrived were too full of the new wonder to allow very much in the way of linguistic exercises, but before the week was out a routine was established. It was different from before because Pamela no longer had to wander around to find Khoka huddling by a fence or a familiar tree. Now that the boy was moving through the village with relative freedom they could rendezvous. In time Khoka learned the pathways and began coming to the lodge to meet Pamela. From there they would go with Prince across the dikes and into fields where neither of them had been before.

"*Cil*," Khoka said as a steady *ki-ki-kitit-wee* floated down to them from above. They were sitting under an enormous banyan tree on the farthest edge of the rice fields. A kestrel soared on fixed wings in a broad circle, scanning the ground below for field mice. Prince lay curled up at Khoka's feet.

"*Cil ache pakhi*," Pamela said, demonstrating that she knew a *cil* was a bird.

"*Hae, pakhi — khoro toro pakhi!*" Khoka revealed, describing the kestrel's swift, darting flight when prey is spotted. They had come that far — they were able to carry on a conversation of sorts. Sometimes it was in Bengali, or *banlae,* sometimes it was in English, but generally a mixture was easier for both. In their world of mixed languages Prince was sometimes known as *Rajputro,* the Bengali equivalent of his original name. He would now answer to either.

"Paamela. Will my eyes ever come?" Khoka asked that question often and caught Pamela off guard every time. Handicapped people can be frustrated but are seldom embarrassed by their afflictions. Any self-consciousness is generally on the part of others.

"I don't know, Khoka. *Ami bolte parbo na.*"

Glenn had been unable to leave the lodge for nearly fifteen hours. The reports coming in seemed to indicate that the herd was about to move again. If they swung south he was in trouble, in danger of losing his chance at them. If they swung north or west he would have them in a good location for launching the operation. Then, just before dusk, the word came. It was north. The herd known as "Likely" was moving in a direct line toward the holding area, where Satwyne on Bolo Bahadur and Oroon on Sabal Kali were waiting.

"Be careful, darling. We need you more than the elephants do. And look out for snakes!"

"I will. Be a good girl. I'll be back or send word by tomorrow afternoon."

"Be a good girl! What are the alternatives in Pukmaranpur?"

With two runners as guides Glenn and Ata started off on the four-mile hike to the holding area. A swollen stream that had been no trouble for the elephants, but which was forbidding to men on foot, forced a detour, and the short march took them over two and a half hours. It was dark when they reached camp. A small fire crackled in a shallow pit and the six men of the *phandi* teams sat huddled around in a circle, the flame-shadows playing soft tricks with their features. *"Adab," "Adab,"* the greeting went around, until each man had greeted them and been greeted in turn.

Glenn sat cross-legged on a mat next to Ata eating rice from a small bowl and picking hard-boiled eggs out of a central pot. He sat back and examined the scene around him. Above them the evening wind was soughing quietly through the trees. Somewhere in the distance a coarse, dry cough intimidated a night bird that was whispering a plaintive *seep seep seepadoo*.

"Chita baghh," Satwyne said. *"Hae,"* the others murmered, *"chita baghh."*

Glenn thought of the leopard out there moving through the forest and felt a slight shiver run through him. He hunched his shoulders against it, and then found himself listening very, very carefully.

You cannot sit quietly in a wild place without becoming a part of the place yourself. A jungle at night particularly absorbs the observer, for it is a whisperer of secrets, a community of powers and mysteries. It is also a place where an elf can become a giant by the simple act of peeling back a shadow. For Glenn it was one of the most exciting and strangely pleasurable experiences of his life. He was out where the animals were, with men whose skill, intelligence and ancient traditions made them masters over the largest terrestrial animals left on this planet. Glenn admired them more than he knew how to express. These men still belonged to the world they lived in. They were not bystanders but participants. What do I belong to, Glenn asked himself. What am I an integral part of?

No one did much sleeping that night, least of all Glenn. At dawn the camp was awake. They ate a simple breakfast of tea and rice in silence while they waited for the first runners to arrive. Glenn looked around at the group sitting quietly by the small fire pit. He couldn't help reflecting how strange it was that some men in the course of their lives come to treat extreme danger with indifference. With the exception of a few score men, anyone faced with the task these men were about to tackle would pale with terror. It is easier to become a United States senator, Glenn thought, than a *phandi*, particularly a *bor phandi*, or top expert, like Satwyne and Oroon, yet their names are in no books, and no newspapers report their doings. Today they will live or die on the job, and few people outside their families will ever know the difference. They are among the most courageous and skilled men in the world, yet there probably aren't a hundred people outside of the Hill

Tracts who even know their profession by name. Some eccentric British lord sails his sailboat across an ocean with half the American Coast Guard tracking him on radar and the British Navy out in force to overfly him and the papers are full of it for weeks.

Part of Glenn's fretting was an effort to mask his own feelings of envy and inadequacy. He wished that he might be half the man that either Satwyne or Oroon was. He had grown up on the periphery of the "Old West" in both time and geography and he still cherished the highly romanticized view of manhood nurtured in that time and place.

The first runner arrived before they had finished breakfast. A second arrived ten minutes later. The herd was less than a mile and a half away. The elephants were feeding in their direction.

The two *koonkis* were ready to go. Their saddle pads were strapped in place and the jute ropes with the nooses the *phandis* would use were coiled and ready. Each *koonki* was to carry two men into action. The third man on each team would remain behind, his work over for the moment. They were the grass-cutters or *kamlas*, the bottom-rung men. It was their job to supply the *koonkis* with fodder and later to perform the same service for the captives.

In a reversal of the method used in normal elephant operations, the *mahouts*, now the second men on the teams, sat to the rear of the pads holding *ankuses*, long goads with which to guide the mounts.

The *phandis*, perched up forward, would be too busy to direct the elephants' movements. Those directions had to come from someone else.

The two teams moved out without ceremony. It was starkly casual. With the exception of an occasional hand signal they would hardly communicate with each other until the first noose was thrown. By some unexplained means, however — and Glenn had heard it described as extrasensory — they would each know what the other was doing and what help was needed. Talking was out of the question. A human voice, even a whisper, is an unnatural sound in the jungle, and a herd with cows and suckling calves moving through dense forest that houses both tigers and leopards is alert to any foreign sound.

Within fifteen minutes the teams made contact. They could hear the herd feeding and from their vantage points high up on the *koonkis'* backs the *phandis* and *mahouts* could see an occasional trunk reach up and search for a special morsel. Also there were the more personal sounds the wild elephants made. The gaseous stomach rumblings known as borborygmus were clear and unmistakable.

Satwyne's *mahout*, Ma, automatically held Bolo Bahadur back. As a male he was likely to cause more suspicion than the female Sabal Kali. He was even likely to be attacked by one of the herd's bulls. The cow, however, would be able to insinuate herself and her riders into the middle of the herd without disturbing the routine of the highly suspicious and often dangerously tense animals.

As Oroon's *mahout*, Rauton, eased Sabal Kali in toward the herd he spotted a young tusker pacing back and forth in a suspicious manner. With almost imperceptible signals he turned Sabal Kali away to approach the herd from another angle. Again, though, he encountered the tusker, who somehow seemed alerted to their intent, and again he had to turn Sabal Kali aside. The tusker was snatching up bunches of debris from the forest floor and throwing them about. He was rocking back and forth on his great forelegs, snapping his ears forward and back and exhaling loudly through his trunk. He took several steps to the right, and then several to the left. He snapped his ears again and blasted air through his trunk, creating a small dust storm at his feet. He took two steps forward, spun around and rushed off into the midst of the herd. Both Oroon and Rauton knew he would be back and would bear careful watching. No one could predict when his clownish display would convert itself into a murderous charge.

Then Oroon saw the cow. She was no more than six feet six at the shoulder but she was unmistakably a *koomeriah*. This cow of the highest caste is one of the best of all working elephants, strong, noble and intelligent. She was their target. She was a young animal, probably one that hadn't yet calved, but she was beautiful. The task that would now occupy all of Rauton's time was getting Sabal Kali close enough to the cow for Oroon to be able to noose her. Oroon hadn't said anything to Rauton, hadn't even signaled to him, but the *mahout* had seen the *koomeriah* at the same time as the *phandi* and had known immediately that as long as that cow was available for a try no other elephant would be of interest.

The cow, unsuspicious, fed calmly at the edge of the herd. She seemed to be particularly attached to an older animal who could very well have been her mother. The two were never very far apart, and both Oroon and Rauton knew that they would have to work their way in between them in order to cut the younger cow out of the herd.

Several more times they were forced to separate from the herd because of the attentions of the nervous young bull. He repeated his threat display twice more and the *phandi* was beginning to find him tiresome.

Although they had seen the *koomeriah* cow before seven in the morning it was almost two o'clock in the afternoon before they finally got close enough to make an approach.

Their patience was rewarded. She stopped to pull some leaves off a high bush and Rauton goaded Sabal Kali forward. Oroon stood on the *koonki's* neck and threw the *phand*. Before the cow knew what had happened it settled over her head and Oroon pulled back hard. The noose was set. The cow immediately spun around and the rope began peeling off the neat pile on Sabal Kali's back. Automatically, without any additional instructions, the *koonki* turned so that the side where the rope was attached to her girth strap was facing the noosed captive. To have allowed the rope to cross her chest or rump would have been to invite a tangle and possible disaster. The *koonki* began sidestepping in toward the bewildered cow who had stopped at the end of the rope. Oroon took in the slack as fast as Sabal Kali presented him with it. The cow stood quietly for a moment trying to understand her predicament, then she took off again. Sabal Kali had to sit back on her haunches to check the flight. Satwyne's *mahout*, Ma, was moving Bolo Bahadur into position between the noosed cow and the rest of the herd. Slowly the two *koonkis* would squeeze her into the position that was necessary to complete the capture.

Satwyne kept his eye on the nervous bull, who was now thoroughly alerted. The rest of the herd seemed unaware of the situation and were strung off in several directions, feeding contentedly. Ma had to maneuver Bolo Bahadur out of the way twice when the bull seemed intent on charging. An angry tusker could impale and kill a *makhna*. Although the men were anxious to get to Oroon's aid as quickly as possible they had to avoid becoming the target of a charge. If the whole herd stampeded in wild confusion mayhem could ensue. It was a critical moment, with disaster a ready potential. In the meantime Sabal Kali was deftly sidestepping to keep the cow in check and to avoid tangling the rope around a tree. Too much pressure was dangerous for the captive; the noose rested on her trachea. If they allowed her to panic she could easily sustain a fatal injury. A wild lunge against the heavy rope while it was in that position would be the equivalent of a monstrous karate chop across the throat.

Finally, Ma was able to elude the tusker and bring Bolo Bahadur up to the captive on the side opposite Sabal Kali. Quietly and steadily Bolo pushed against the cow and began easing her toward Oroon, who was furiously working to take in the slack and twirl it back onto a neat pile, where it would be free to peel off again without tangling if the captive decided to make another attempt at freedom.

The maneuvering went on for nearly two hours. The tension didn't slacken for a single moment. Both teams had to concentrate on their own strategy, the cow's movements, and the activities of the herd in general. Working in concert they finally managed to separate her from the herd. They could hear the dozen or more other elephants breaking through some brush about a quarter of a mile away. The nervous young tusker trumpeted once. It was a sad sound, a confused lament rather than a challenge or an expression of fury. The men stopped to listen but it was not repeated. The jungle swallowed the herd, now short one beautiful young cow.

The two *koonkis* pinned the *koomeriah* between them, making any further struggle on her part useless. Bracing with their outside legs, they leaned in, putting their combined weight on her flanks. She was already exhausted from her early struggles and went to her knees. She was only down for a moment, though, and was quickly on her feet again. She reached up with her trunk to explore Bola Bahadur's head. Satwyne smacked it smartly and she withdrew it. Her trunk was the weapon the *phandis* feared most for with it she could grasp a man and bring him within reach of her feet. She tried the same trick with Oroon, who also delivered a blow to the sensitive slender end of her trunk. Again she withdrew it.

Satwyne dismounted from Bolo Bahadur and went around to shackle the cow's hind legs while Oroon slipped off Sabal Kali's off side and adjusted the noose around the captive's neck with a check-rope that would keep her from strangling herself. While the two *phandis* were on the ground the *mahouts* urged their mounts to lean in harder, to pin the cow so that she was all but paralyzed. Crushed by the two trained elephants and whacked painfully on the trunk every time she tried to lift it, she was defenseless. She coiled her trunk as tightly as she could and hummed and moaned her despair. Her eyes were wide with terror as she was touched by human hands for the first time.

Satwyne maneuvered the rope around her hind legs, tying a figure eight or *degi* hitch. Later, a similar hitch called a *banda* would be fitted to her forelegs.

With surprising speed the cow was lashed between the two *koonkis*, who were then free to ease the pressure and start slowly walking her toward the *pilkhana*. There her training would commence. Within three weeks she would be expected to carry a *mahout* on her own neck, without a *koonki* in attendance. Her spirit would be broken that quickly, and that quickly she would come to accept the fact that there were masters who were to rule her destiny. She would come to know that pain was associated with misbehavior. She would learn to follow fifteen one-word commands without any display of reluctance. Then, and only then, the brutalizing by man and *koonki* would stop, and for the rest of her life she would be treated not only well but with affection and respect. She was on her way to becoming a trained working elephant.

Once the cow was secured in the *pilkhana* area, Kala and Khada, the two grass-cutters of the *phandi* teams, took over. They brought fodder to her, although it would be a day or two before she would eat, and left tins of water where she could reach them. They poured hot water over the *koonkis*'s backs and rubbed them down, then fed and watered them. They mounted watch on the captive while Satwyne, Ma, Oroon and Rauton returned to the campfire, too exhausted even to discuss the day's activities.

Glenn instinctively knew that these men were too far along in their profession to require a cheering section. They had done what they had set out to do, and had laid their lives on the line in doing it. The fact that they had succeeded and survived was enough.

10

The Hunt

Glenn's incredible luck held; the two teams were able to cut out and secure a *makhna* before noon on the second day. He was a handsome animal, standing a little over nine feet at the shoulder. While not a true *koomeriah*, he was a fine *dwasala* and appeared to be sensible and even-tempered although apparently immensely powerful. He did not struggle long because the heavy jute rope was cutting his wind off, but twice after the squeeze was started by the two *koonkis* he was able to sweep the powerful Bolo Bahadur aside with a shove of his hip.

The nobility of an elephant is not gauged by the struggle he puts up when captured. In most cases, violent struggling is more a sign of hysteria than of outrage or bravery. The more stable an elephant's nature, the more likely it is that he will hold back to assess the situation before starting to thrash around. What the elephant doesn't understand, of course, is that once his captors are allowed to take the first step his days of freedom are over.

Noosing and securing two fine wild elephants in a little less than thirty hours is a record accomplishment for two *koonki* teams working a *mela shikar* operation in heavy forest — so Ata assured Glenn.

While Kala and Khada attended to the *koonkis* and mounted guard over the captives the *mahouts* and *phandis* went down to the stream and bathed. Their muscles ached with the tension they had been under since making contact early the previous morning, and they were lathered in sweat. The sweet, cool water flowed over them as they lay almost totally submerged on the sandy bottom, making appreciative noises and calling to each other in cryptic Bengali, laughing at each other's comments about the operations they had just completed. The foolish young tusker who had put on such a show took the brunt of their jokes. They called him *Idur*, the Bengali word for "mouse." The fact that he had put on such a show without attempting to carry through his threats earned him their disdain. He would have been a nervous and unreliable animal in captivity, they assured each other, and it was a good thing that Glennsahib hadn't wanted a tusker. They then went on to discuss the fine qualities of the animals they had taken, particularly those of the beautiful young *koomeriah* cow. Their visitor from Kansas sat on the bank watching them and listening to their conversation. He understood almost nothing of what they were saying, but somehow that didn't matter. It was like being in the locker room with a team that has just won the world series, Glenn thought. He felt highly privileged.

Through Ata, Glenn asked the *phandis* to name his elephants for him. He told them that it would bring the captives good luck to be named by the men who outwitted them. It was the kind of belief the *phandis* could easily accept, and after a conference they suggested Begam Bahar for the young cow and Sikander for the *makhna*, both names having belonged to well-remembered *koonkis* long since dead. And so the first two elephants in the experimental agricultural herd got their names.

Since the capture was made close to Pukmaranpur it was decided that it would be worth the effort to move the trainees in to the outskirts of the village. It would be easier to maintain them there and would enable the crews to live in the village without having to face an eight-mile trek each day. Glenn went on ahead to establish a new *pilkhana* and to arrange for a supply of food and water.

When he reached the lodge Liz was waiting for him. Runners had brought in the news of the quick captures, but she was anxious to see for herself that her husband hadn't disappeared underfoot. She could tell by the look in his eye that his adventure with the *phandi* teams had been important for him. There was a shine, a gleam about him that came when he was stimulated; when he had recaptured, even briefly, something of what every man loses the farther he gets away from his youth. She recognized it and was happy for him. He was dirty, he smelled like an elephant himself, and he needed a shave. Funny, she mused, this is when a man is most attractive and, in beholding him, a woman most a woman. She kept to herself the fact that she had gone into a fit of depression shortly after Glenn left and had been all but immobilized by a deep sense of foreboding. The cloud hadn't begun to lift until the arrival of the runners. She had managed to pull herself together by the time Glenn arrived.

Each day Pamela and Khoka expanded their horizons a little more. There were endless paths and trails in the square mile of territory that was roughly included in the village. These paths led off to various fishing and bathing spots along the river, to open fields and to the forest. There were intersecting paths that cut between the major trails, and the complex as a whole could be extremely confusing. Khoka, of course, had followed none of these trails, and Pamela very few before Prince's arrival. With Prince to lead them, though, they felt increasingly bold, and although they had never yet quite broken the rule that Pamela's mother had established about "wandering off into the jungle" they had come very close to it.

On the day of the second elephant's capture they were exploring a new trail that ran northward parallel to the river. Khoka had heard about an ancient temple or *mondir* in the forest and they hoped to be able to find it without having to travel far enough to be guilty of an infraction of the rules — at least not too guilty. Pamela walked beside Khoka, and Prince moved ahead at a pace sensibly adjusted to the terrain. He had the uncanny ability to judge the speed a blind person is capable of under varying surface conditions. Khoka didn't establish the pace, Prince did, and Khoka adapted himself to it.

They hadn't gone more than half a mile before the trail began to narrow, curving away from the river and descending into what once had been an adjacent stream but was now a great slash in the earth filled with heavy growth. It was a dark place, where dark things could happen.

Except for an occasional birdcall it was almost dead silent. Once a crashing behind a screen of vegetation signaled the departure of a wild boar, but then the silence returned. Like the humidity down in the airless draw, the very lack of sound was oppressive. It seemed to close in from all sides, threatening suffocation or worse. The overhead growth was so thick that the measurable light was less than a quarter of what it was a hundred yards away on the river. Interstices between the trees were often so swathed in shadows that it appeared to be night. Where light did penetrate it came in shafts: bright, narrow avenues of sun through which butterflies and other insects flew for brief flashing moments of glory.

It is a strange characteristic of human beings that when they are in a quiet place they tend to whisper. Silence seems to be something they hesitate to dispel. People who do not whisper when the natural world around them does are generally thought of as boors by their fellowmen.

Pamela and Khoka whispered their brief, bilingual messages to each other. Prince had slowed his pace when the trail began to descend into the cut. Almost silently the two children followed. Khoka leaned forward so as not to lose the handle on Prince's harness.

Suddenly, Prince stopped. He braked with his front legs as his whole body stiffened. The sudden tension transmitted itself back along the handle to Khoka's sensitive hands. An exploratory rumble started deep in the shepherd's throat.

Pamela had a swift, overwhelming premonition that something terrible was about to happen. She could see the hair along Prince's spine and across his shoulders stiffen. His lips rolled back in a snarl. Without any other warning he was on his hind legs pushing backwards against Khoka. Both Pamela and Khoka, who were standing very close, were caught off balance and thrown to the ground. Prince stood over them, snarling furiously. The sound that began in his throat seemed to slip backwards into his chest and then to issue from his entire body. He was rigid with fury. The children lay paralyzed on the ground, too frightened to cry or call out. Slowly Prince advanced toward the edge of the trail. He went into a half-crouch, the deep echo of his fury unabated. Then Pamela saw it, at first only as a slight movement behind a trailside bush.

Again a branch moved and then the whole bush seemed to open like two halves of a book. Khoka of course heard only the sounds but Pamela saw it all and it seemed to happen in a dreamlike kind of slow motion. The bush parted, the face appeared, then the shoulders, then the long yellow flanks with the prominent stripes. The tigress arched out of the bush without any apparent effort and as Prince reared back she caught him in the barrel of his chest and continued on across the trail with her prize dangling from her jaws. Prince whimpered only once before the tigress crushed his chest. They could hear her movements for only a moment or two and then it was silent again, except for Pamela's whimpering and Khoka's soft moans of despair.

"*Baghh,*" Pamela gasped between sobs. "*Baghh,*"

she said again, trying to make Khoka understand that it had been a tiger.

He still didn't comprehend the enormity of his loss and was crawling around on all fours crying for his dog: "Rajputro. Rajputro. Print. Print..."

"*Na, na, Khoka! Rajputro . . . nihoto . . . baghh . . . nihoto . . . nihoto!*"

She was trying desperately to explain to him that the tiger had killed his dog, but he couldn't or wouldn't understand. Finally he came to the edge of the trail and crawled halfway into a bush. He fell back onto the path and desperately called, "*Rajputro, Rajputro!*"

Pamela was sitting beside him, too numb to move, too dulled by shock to help. They sat on the trail, side by side, hunched over and weeping, shaking with terror.

Two fishermen cleaning their catch at the river were the first to see the children. They looked up and saw them moving up out of the forest trail like two sleepwalkers. Pamela was in the lead with one arm stretched out behind her. Khoka had both of his hands clamped on her wrist as he stumbled along with his head thrown back, wailing softly to himself. Pamela was staring straight ahead, apparently possessed by a memory or a vision that was still before her eyes. Sensing immediately that something was seriously wrong, the fishermen darted up the bank to the children. In answer to their urgent questioning Pamela repeated softly, *"baghh."*

The younger man asked hesitantly, *"Rajputro?"* *"Nihoto — baghh nihoto."* Her grammar was bad but the meaning was clear. The fishermen sucked in their breath and started after the children as they continued their somnambulant walk toward the village plaza. As they moved forward people stopped what they were doing and stared. That a pall of tragedy hung over them was apparent at a glance. The younger fisherman walked behind them, explaining what had happened. A tiger had taken *Rajputro!* A tiger had killed the dog who was the eyes of the boy! Word spread ahead of them as they moved across the plaza, Pamela still pulling the whimpering Khoka along. A small group gathered around them but no one knew what to do. A path remained opened, and the children passed through. Pamela, apparently as unseeing as Khoka, did not turn her head.

The news quickly reached the lodge, and moments after the children entered the village center, Liz and Glenn were racing down the path toward the school. They had heard only that a tiger attack had occurred and that Pamela was involved. Their terror grew as they ran and when they burst into the plaza and saw their daughter standing there intact Liz let go with a shout of release. They almost knocked the children over as they embraced them. Even in her parents' arms Pamela didn't lose control. She quietly buried her face in her father's chest. Liz clutched Khoka to her and under her influence he seemed to settle down. A crowd had gathered around them and stood watching silently. Manik appeared and knelt beside Glenn.

"Manik. A tiger got the dog. Send someone to Satwyne. He should be here."

Satwyne was supervising the security hitches on Begam Bahar at the new training area at the western end of the village when he heard what had happened. He slid off Bolo Bahadur, nodded to Ma, who took charge, and ran toward the lodge. When he arrived Glenn and Liz were trying their best to work the children out of their shock. Khoka seemed to regain a measure of control first but then Pamela whimpered aloud and he began to sob again. Glenn gently picked the boy up in his arms and carried him off into the next room. It was as he was laying him down on the bed that Satwyne entered. He knelt and whispered in his son's ear. Khoka rolled over and threw his arm around his father's neck and spoke to him softly. Glenn slipped out of the room as the boy poured out his sorrow.

When Glenn returned to the living room Ata was standing there.

"I'm so relieved. I'd heard that Pamela had been taken! My God!"

"I guess it was close but the tiger was after the dog, not the kids."

"All of the jungle cats are dog-eaters. They are seldom man-eaters. Still it was too close!"

Glenn saw Liz stand up and move away from Pamela. He saw her shoulders shake and her head tip forward. He went over to her and put his arms around her. She turned to him and looked up into his eyes.

"Glenn? What are we doing here? What is important enough to put our daughter's life in jeopardy?"

Ata, seeing what was coming, went off to the other room, ostensibly to see if there was anything he could do for Khoka and Satwyne. He was surprised to see the boy alone. He knelt beside the bed and speaking softly asked Khoka where his father was. In a dry, emotionless voice the boy answered that his father had promised to kill the *baghh*.

Ata hurried back into the main room. "Khoka says his father has gone after the tiger."

"Alone? Does he have a gun?"

Glenn turned and ran into the central room of the lodge. Two pegs stood empty where his .300 H&H Magnum always hung. He ran across to a chest of drawers and throwing some papers aside located two boxes of cartridges. Ripping the ends off he emptied them onto a table. Twenty long coppery tubes slipped out of each box.

"My God!" he murmured aloud. "Ata! Ata! Come

quickly! Satwyne has gone after that tiger with my Magnum. I never keep anything loaded in the house. He's gone after it with an empty rifle!"

Glenn raced across the room and pulled his 12-gauge pump off its pegs and got a box of shells from the drawer that hung sagging where he had left it. He rammed three shells into the tube under the barrel while he shouted to Ata to find out from Pamela where the attack had taken place. Ata raced back to where Pamela was sitting in a chair quietly looking out of a window.

Glenn kissed Liz quickly on the forehead. "Don't let either of them out of your sight, and if any runners come with bad news don't let Khoka find it out that way. If we don't find Satwyne before he finds that tiger, Khoka's going to be an orphan."

Before Liz could answer Glenn and Ata were gone. She began to shake. For a moment she was certain she would let go, but somehow she hung on and even forced a wan little smile as she walked into the room where Pamela was sitting. She took her daughter by the hand. Pamela responded by standing and throwing her arms around her mother. Liz hugged her daughter to her, the line of her jaw set and her eyes glistening in anger and frustration.

"Come on, darling. Let's not leave Khoka alone."

Ata was familiar with the trail where the attack had taken place and led Glenn to it without hesitation. As they started down toward the dry riverbed the same gloom that had surrounded the children only an hour before enveloped them. They ran side by side until the trail narrowed; then Glenn moved into the lead. He called out for Satwyne several times but there was no answer, not even an echo. He didn't notice the small signs that showed where the attack had taken place and passed them while still staring down into the gloom. It was deeper now because the sun had slipped behind the hill to the west of the cut. Ata, however, saw the broken branches to the left of the trail. They marked the spot where the tiger had broken through with the dog in her jaws. He called to Glenn as he knelt to examine a single drop of blood on a broken leaf.

Together they penetrated the thick growth behind the bush. In a mud patch near a place where a small spring bubbled to the surface they saw a pug mark, the clear, unmistakably fresh imprint of a tiger's paw and near it the imprint of a naked human foot, fresher still.

"He's found the trail."

Without hesitation the two men set off in the direction the two prints were pointing. The land fell away in front of them and they fought their way down through extremely thick cover. Glenn broke through the wall of vegetation first, with Ata panting directly behind him. They were pouring with sweat and both of them were covered with scratches from the thick tangle through which they had charged. If

Satwyne came this way, Glenn thought, this stuff closed up behind him like the Red Sea!

They were standing in a small clearing beside a narrow brook that moved slowly between two strips of mud three feet wide at the very bottom of the cut. On either side of them the vegetation rolled upward in layers and billows curving inward until it completely blocked out the sky. The jungle around them was bathed in a green-black light, and occasional white flowers, enormous blossoms several inches across, stood out against the deep, dark foliage like small spotlights. It was utterly silent. They looked around them and had identical reactions. With cover only three feet away on either side, cover into which they could not see, *anything* could watch them, and attack them at will. An army could be hiding only inches away.

Jack-ae jack-ae jackae-ae, the musical, almost obscenely cheerful call of a *dnarkaak* or jackdaw drifted down to them with startling brilliance, and then the wood fell silent again. Glenn began examining the mud flats beside the streams. If either the tiger or Satwyne had passed that way their prints would be certain to show. Ata knelt beside him and whispered breathlessly into his ear.

"This stream opens out into a *dal bheel* further down. The grass is over a man's head. It is impossible to pursue a tiger there without beaters and elephants."

Glenn knew he was right. The heavy grass-covered

swamp Ata was describing was suicide for a man pursuing a tiger on foot. The cat would be invisible only inches away, but with its keen hearing it would be able to move around and take the man whenever it suited its fancy to do so.

Then they saw it. A clear pug mark, then another. The tiger had come down the east side of the draw, crossed the stream and gone into the cover on the far side, heading up toward the hills. It hadn't headed for the swamp. A foot away from the pug mark was the equally clear imprint of Satwyne's foot. The poor devil, Glenn shuddered, he went into that cover with an empty gun!

Glenn looked up into the solid wall of vegetation that rose above them. He looked at Ata who was examining the prints. Again Ata whispered, "A female, I think. Not a very big one. She's carrying the dog too far! She must have a cub and be anxious to get back to it."

A female with a cub! Glenn felt the cold premonition of tragedy steal over him: Satwyne didn't stand a chance! He jumped across the stream and began looking for a way through the green tangle. There wasn't one. Taking a deep breath he plunged in blindly. The brush and vines clung to his clothes and several times he was completely clear of the ground, literally creeping through and across the brush, unable to find a place to put his foot down. He finally managed to crash through and fall to the ground. He could hear Ata struggling along behind him. He waited until his companion collapsed at his side. Ata's face was a mass of welts and cuts. Glenn could see where individual branches and thorny stems had cruelly lashed him, leaving an angry red criss-cross pattern. His own face felt as if it were on fire.

As they started to their feet Ata pointed to a bush about ten feet up the slope from where they had collapsed. A piece of white cotton hung on a branch. They were still on Satwyne's trail, and he presumably was still on the tiger's track.

They pushed up the steeply rising slope. In several places shallow streams flowed down the bank, adding slick mud to their problems. In one particularly steep place Glenn reached up to grab a branch when he felt Ata grasp him by the belt and pull him back. He nearly fell over backwards and felt a flare of anger. He checked himself and as he turned he was frozen by the look on Ata's face. Ata nodded past him toward the ledge he had been trying to attain.

No more than five feet away was an enormous king cobra, at least eighteen feet long. It was pale olive with faint yellow chevron-shaped bands along its entire length. Glenn had seen pictures of them and recognized it immediately. The king cobra, only distantly related to the common cobra, is the largest venomous snake in the world. An eighteen-foot specimen can deliver one hundred and twenty times the amount of venom necessary to paralyze and kill a normal man. And Glenn stood less than a third of its body length away from it.

The snake had raised the top four feet of its body slightly off the ground and was poised rigidly, staring straight at Glenn with small lidless black eyes. Occasionally a pale-pink forked tongue darted out from a hole that remained at the front of the snake's mouth even when its jaws were shut. The movement of the tongue, itself looking like a two-headed serpent, was the only sign that the snake was alive. It continued to stare directly into Glenn's face and he realized with horror that he was beginning to feel faint. He could hear his heart drumming in his temples and feel small twitches on his neck and throat. He felt cool, despite the oppressive heat of the airless draw, and he began to feel more and more detached from the reality of the whole episode. He felt as if he were floating away from the scene, far off to the side, safe from any danger, watching the whole thing happen to some-one else.

For what seemed like an eternity the snake remained fixed. Glenn fought to keep his wits and kept telling himself that he wasn't going to let go, that he was going to hold on even if it took the snake a century to make up its mind. Had he been only a few feet further away he would have risked snapping his shotgun up and letting fly with it. But he was holding it at a trail and long before he could bring it up to where he could reach the trigger the snake

could hit him. In fact, he knew that the slightest
movement of any kind could cause the snake to
strike. A strike at that distance for a snake eighteen
feet long would be little more than a snapping motion. Glenn realized that the reptile had them pinned
down for as long as it suited it.

Slowly the snake began to rise higher off the
ground. At first Glenn thought he was seeing things
but then realized it was true: it was slowly raising the
forepart of its body, and the ribs behind its head were
beginning to spread, displaying the characteristic
cobra hood. Glenn could hear Ata, immediately behind him, involuntarily suck in his breath. Higher
and higher the cobra rose until the first four feet of
his body were sticking almost straight up. The cruel
little head arched over at the top of the hood like the
crest on a wave. The tongue flicked in and out, in and
out, and Glenn thought he was going to have to
scream, if only to relieve the tension that had built up
inside of him. The snake, being deaf, wouldn't hear
it, but Glenn decided against it. He would be apt to
move, and then, too, he might startle Ata into moving, which would be as bad.

Then, inexplicably, with an audible plop, the
snake twisted its body, pivoted at the point where it
left the ground and hit the matted debris on the floor
of the jungle. It slithered past the two men, passing
them at a distance of no more than three feet. It took
an eternity for the full eighteen feet to pass and as

the slender tail slipped out of sight behind a bush Glenn felt his stomach tighten and a wave of nausea sweep over him. He began to retch and then vomited. He could hear Ata doing the same thing behind him.

They recovered at about the same time and started forward again, up the slope, past the snake's ledge. As they went forward Glenn's mind cleared and the urgency of Satwyne's predicament returned to him in full force. Once again they were beating their way up the slope as fast as their exhausted bodies would respond.

The woods were thinning out and ahead they could see pale light shining through the trees. They pushed harder and finally made it into a small clearing. Across the clearing the ground continued to rise and was becoming rocky. Small outcroppings were topped by larger ones. It was almost dusk and Glenn knew that the failing light increased the hazard to Satwyne and themselves by a very large margin. Stopping for only a few deep breaths he pushed on up past the first outcropping. He could hear Ata sigh heavily and start up after him.

Glenn heard it first, then Ata — a rock rolling down the slope above them. They heard it hit several times, then fall into some brush where it came to rest. They quickened their pace, rounded an outcropping that was projecting too far out from the slope for them to negotiate, and stopped dead in their tracks. Satwyne was fifteen yards to their left. He was facing up the slope directly beneath a tigress perched on another large rocky prominence. She was down with her belly against the rock, her tail lashing. For a brief second the whole scene was suspended somewhere between reality and nightmare. Nothing moved, not time itself.

Glenn could see the tigress digging in with her hind feet, getting the purchase for her spring. Faster than he would have thought possible he swung the shotgun up to his shoulder and pressed the trigger. He barely heard the explosion, and pumping furiously with his left arm he fired again, and then again. The tigress never left the rock. She slumped down with her head dangling over, her tongue lolling. The face of the rock was slowly covered with a sheet of blood as the tigress's body emptied itself through the massive, gaping wounds that the full-choked loads of buckshot had made in her side. The third shot went wild but the first two had all but cut the great striped cat in half.

Satwyne never got the rifle to his shoulder. He had been momentarily transfixed when he found himself staring directly into the cat's face, and that was when Glenn and Ata had rounded the rock.

What the race against time and the episode with the king cobra hadn't taken out of Glenn, the last-minute confrontation with the tigress had. He slumped to the ground, completely spent. He could hear Satwyne coming toward him and thought he heard him speak in an angry voice. He looked up slowly to see Satwyne glaring down at him. Before he could comprehend the situation Ata reached forward and snatched the rifle away from the *phandi*. He worked the bolt open and handed the rifle back to Satwyne, who stood open-mouthed staring down into the empty chamber. Glenn was too tired to speak and let his head sag forward onto his knees. He could hear or at least sense Satwyne slowly sinking to the ground beside him. He felt the *phandi's* hand rest gently on his arm and heard him murmur what he was sure were the man's apology and thanks. Without lifting his head Glenn reached out with one hand and squeezed the *phandi's* upper arm.

"Anytime, Satwyne, any old time at all. The pleasure was all mine!"

Glenn sighed and rolled over backwards, staring straight up into the sky. I think I'll just lie here until I die, he thought, I really don't think I'll ever move again.

Ata sat for a while and then moved up onto the ledge to examine the body of the tigress. Too bad, he remarked to himself, that the shotgun had ruined the pelt. Two enormous jagged holes showed where the blasts had torn into her, shredding her tissue and bones. As he knelt over the still, striped body, Ata heard a scraping noise behind him. He whirled and saw a small, round copy of the tigress pawing at the body of the dog lying just inside the cave entrance.

It was obviously a very young cub. Its pale, creamy blue eyes hadn't been open more than a few days. It was a male, and as Ata had guessed earlier, it had been the reason the tigress hadn't stopped to eat near the site of her kill. The cub was far too young to be on meat but the tigress had obviously been nervous about leaving it alone.

Satwyne grasped the spitting ball of fury by the scruff of the neck and jerked it off the ground. For one terrible moment Glenn thought he was going to bash it down the rocky face. He called to him to wait, and as Ata translated he asked the *phandi* if he thought Khoka would like to have the cub? It was a quick move, almost a reflexive one, to keep the cub from being killed. Although resentful of what had happened to the children's dog, Glenn had been a conservationist too long not to have a philosophical attitude toward all natural predators. Satwyne thought for a minute and nodded his head affirmatively. He held the struggling cub at arm's length and cocked his head to examine it. He explained to Glenn, through Ata, that the villagers wouldn't tolerate having it around very long. But there would be time enough to worry about that later.

Passing the cub to Ata, Satwyne ripped free part of his tattered *lungi*. He deftly tied it into a sack about the size of a pillow case and held it open to receive the furious cub. He secured the top and gently laid it across his shoulder just as a small claw came through the cloth and found his neck. Ata found a short pole and they tied the sack to it.

As they started down off the ledge Glenn remembered that it had been Ata who had grabbed him by the belt and kept him from blundering into the king cobra. Ata was ahead of him, easing down the slope. He called after him.

"Ata. Thank you."

Ata looked back up at him with a puzzled look on his face. It took him a moment, then he smiled.

"My pleasure, Glenn, any old time at all."

Then Satwyne turned and looked back up at Glenn.

"Glennsaheb. Tank."

Glenn smiled and they started for home, the tiger cub dangling from the pole, spitting with rage and fright. The bodies of Prince and his assassin lay on the ledge, waiting for time and the scavengers to finish the episode by returning their substance to the earth.

11

Sarang

Neither Pamela nor Khoka had entirely recovered from shock when the tiger cub entered their lives. Quite suddenly, even before Prince was properly a thing of the past, he was there, absorbing them, delighting them, drawing them out.

In the first few hours of his captivity the cub was totally unmanageable, and although very young he was capable of inflicting painful injury. It took brute strength to hold him and quick reflexes to avoid his slashing slaps and bites.

Liz managed to fashion a bottle and nipple arrangement out of some spare parts left behind by the tractor people and within a few hours of his capture the cub was feeding. He struggled at first, but before long he took his bottle while sitting contentedly on any available lap. His capacity for both food and attention seemed limitless, and the children took turns holding him and allowing him to grasp the bottle with his forepaws. He always started his feeding the same way, hunched down on his belly with the forepart of his body arched back. Liz showed the children how to hold the bottle high with the end almost straight down so that he didn't get a lot of air with the goat milk they had started him on. Before each feeding was half over, though, the cub would roll over on his back and allow his stomach to be rubbed while he sucked greedily on his bottle, still grasping at it with his front paws. In very short order there was a whole new love affair going. It would be a long time before Prince's hold on them would ease but undeniably, as predicted by Glenn, the cub would help.

Khoka, to whom the cub rightly belonged, asked Pamela to name it for him and without thinking she answered "Sarang." She had heard the word or one like it and although she didn't know its meaning it had a jungly sound that seemed to suit the little tiger. Actually the word she was thinking of was *sareyng*, the title of the launch captain who had brought them up the river from Kaptai. No one questioned her on

the etymology of her choice and the name Sarang
was adopted.

If Khoka and Pamela were totally absorbed by
their new pet, Glenn was as heavily committed to the
business of training his new charges. The makeshift
pilkhana consisted of four heavy poles buried deep in
the ground and tamped with rock debris. Each elephant was tethered to two poles with heavy jute
ropes. Elephants are virtually twenty-four-hour feeders. Shifts of attendants kept fresh fodder available
within their reach at all times. They were watered
regularly: the heaviest task of all since they could
not yet be taken to the river. Every gallon of water
they drank — and the total amounted to hundreds
of pounds of dead weight — had to be carried up the
steep bank from the river, across the village and out
through the rice paddies. It was exhausting work and
it required constant supervision. The men used for
this menial detail were not the best workers in the
village and a breakdown in supervision inevitably
meant a shortage of water at the *pilkhana*.

The most colorful parts of the training were the
nightly song sessions. They seemed to epitomize the
whole tradition of elephant catching and elephant
training. Night after night Glenn and Liz wandered
down the dark trails to the *pilkhana* to watch Satwyne,
Oroon and their relief *mahouts* perform the ritual.
Fires were kept burning in pits near the tethered cap-

tives. The elephants stood in the phantom light weaving back and forth, swishing their ears and rolling and unrolling their trunks. Their movement was incessant and made a soft sandpapery noise. The *phandis* and the *mahouts* stood beside the animals, rubbing them with branches while singing to them in soft Bengali phrases. The words of the songs, although based on traditional ideas, were composed on the spot and went on endlessly in a lilting singsong pattern. Mostly the songs told the elephants how brave and fine and handsome they were and told them of the good care they could expect. There was constant body contact between the elephants and the men who leaned against their flanks while they caressed them. Occasionally they would duck under the elephants or reach up and touch them with the flat of the hand.

The area was suffused with the mixed smells of elephant dung, crushed sweet elephant grass, burning wood, cooking rice, and the sweat of the elephant men who, working in shifts, kept up the hypnotic chanting twenty-four hours a day. Liz and Glenn stood off to the side watching the endless performance for hours, entranced by the sights, the sounds and the smells.

Liz put an arm around her husband. "I can't explain it, but it is one of the most hauntingly beautiful things I have ever seen."

It's the breakthrough, Glenn mused. She has finally

made herself a part of it. She has stopped fighting and is looking for the positive side of it. "I feel it, too."

"I hope this place never changes! I hope and pray that your experiment works out. It would be a crime for them to come back here with their stupid machinery, ever!"

The singing and the chanting had its purpose, of course. The elephants were never allowed to sleep and were kept in a state of exhaustion, night and day. Their power to resist slowly crumbled and the constant touching made the presence of and contact with man a natural rather than a frightening experience. Both animals had learned within the first twenty-four hours to keep their trunks out of the way. They were struck painfully every time they attempted to get them near one of their trainers. At first the captives reacted frantically when they were approached and particularly when they were touched. As their reactions became less and less violent the men took more and more liberties with them.

To say that the captives were in a trance may stretch the point slightly, but their condition was something akin to that. They were constantly surrounded by men, watered and fed by men, touched and massaged by men, and they were never without the sound of human voices nearby, often right beside their enormous heads. Sometime back near the beginning of man's two-thousand-year association with these great animals this ritual evolved. It still works as no other system does, and Glenn's first two elephants slowly buckled under its influence. Within seventy-two hours after their capture they were taking food from the hands of their new masters and allowing them to approach without shying.

On the fifth day Begam Bahar, the beautiful cow *koomeriah*, was lashed between Sabal Kali and Bolo Bahadur. Her front and then her hind legs were freed from the tethering posts and the two-*koonki* stage of her training began. Her body was laced with an intricate pattern of jute ropes designed to restrict her movement. With Satwyne walking in front with a long *ankus* to punish her for any misdemeanor, she was moved out. They walked her back and forth, endlessly talking to her, praising her, turning her on command, and making her back up. At one point Ma, who was to be her *mahout,* slipped over from the back of Bolo Bahadur and carefully took up his position on her neck. She panicked and sank to her knees with a shrill blast from her trunk. The *ankus* was laid on heavily and the *koonkis* dragged her forward so rapidly that she had to walk or lose the skin on her forelegs. She was beaten when she attempted to sweep Ma off with her trunk and before the day was over she permitted him to get on and off without protest.

The process was repeated with the *makhna* Sikander, who reacted in much the same way as the young cow. Again that night they were kept awake with chanting and massaging and the following morning they were each walked again with *mahouts* on their necks. This time there was no resistance at all and they began to respond to the signals, both vocal and physical. The *mahouts* spoke their commands, which were followed immediately by the *koonkis'* dragging the captives after them. As this was accomplished the *mahouts* drove their toes in behind the captive's ears. Where necessary the sharp hooked end of the *ankus* was employed and in time running sores developed. Native remedies were applied to keep the wounds from becoming infected but they remained tender and vulnerable to the goading the elephants received when either exhibited any reluctance.

Glenn hated the brutal aspects of this training but was wise enough to keep his misgivings to himself. This was the way it had always been done and would continue to be done for the relatively few years left in which the art could be practiced. The progress made was astounding, and after ten days the captives were going out lashed to just one *koonki* with a *mahout* sitting in position. The captives no longer waited to be dragged but were responding themselves. Begam Bahar was the better pupil of the two and showed an uncanny knack for avoiding punishment. She did whatever she could to resist as long as she knew she could get away with it. Once she was punished for something she never tried it again. Sikander, on the other hand, took some bad beatings before he finally learned the futility of resistance. More and more the men who worked the captives put themselves in positions that would have been suicide had the elephants been wild or freshly caught. The animals' spirits had been broken and the thought of attacking their captors never seemed to occur to them.

Glenn and Liz were fascinated witnesses to the whole operation from the beginning. On occasion Pamela came down to the *pilkhana* to watch. Although she was as enthralled as her parents, there were other things on her mind. She and Khoka had their own wild animal to train.

The developments in Sarang were not as dramatic as those easily seen by watching Sikander and Begam Bahar, but there were definite changes that came over the cub. He not only learned not to attack the small boy and girl who cherished him, but learned to love them in return. If either of them entered the room they were assured of a greeting as demonstrative as the cub's hate and fear had once been. He rubbed against their legs, stood clumsily on his own hind legs in an effort to climb into their laps and would sleep beside either of them for hours on end, contentedly sucking on their fingers. Liz provided a ball of twine that became a favored toy. Sarang would bat it back and forth with Pamela until at last, overflowing with enthusiasm, he demolished it with a ludicrous display of snarling and spitting. The children were never with him without being reduced to tears of helpless laughter.

Khoka was able to follow the action, of course, only with the help of Pamela. As they rolled about on the ground with their pet, laughing and calling to each other, the language barrier that remained between them began its final collapse. If their conscious efforts to learn each other's language had been successful as far as it went, their unconscious exchange was even more effective. The number of thoughts they could not convey became fewer each day.

As the weeks passed, Sarang graduated from goat's milk to goat's milk with rice gruel. The bottle gave way to the bowl and he continued to grow.

He very quickly passed out of the little cub stage and began to show signs of his adolescence. His legs grew longer and his flanks less round. His disposition gave no sign of changing but his size was increasing.

One day Glenn and Liz sat on the lodge's veranda watching Pamela and Khoka playing with their pet.

"How much longer can this go on, Glenn? I hate to think of separating them."

"I don't know, honey, but the villagers will make that decision. He is a tiger, after all, and pretty soon he's going to be a big one."

"Do you think there's any danger of him turning? I don't like to think of what he could do even now."

"He sure doesn't act like he's going to turn, but someday he may remember that he's a wild animal.

I just don't know. I don't know how we can make them give him up, either. So help me, he saved Khoka's sanity!"

The discussion of Sarang's ultimate fate came up often and followed the same pattern each time. There was never a resolution. It was repeatedly stated as a problem, but that was as far as it went.

Sarang gave no sign that he would ever turn. He gave every indication of being as emotionally bound to the two children as they were to him. He followed them like a dog, lay down with them for afternoon naps when the heat was at its worst, and paddled through flooded paddy fields, enjoying the noise and the splashing as much as they did. He was gentle in all circumstances and no matter how rough the play became he never put out a claw or bared his teeth. He became such a familiar fixture around the lodge that the adults found themselves talking to him as if he were a person. He was responsive to almost anyone who would give him any attention but he reserved a special kind of affection for his two youngest friends. At their approach he would start his enormous purring sounds and rub against their legs as he had done when he was a kitten.

The houseboys had been raised at the edge of the jungle and had heard of times when man-eaters terrorized the countryside. Somehow, though, even they overcame their cultivated dread of *baghh* and automatically stooped to pat him when he passed. On several occasions when Sarang made a pest of himself in the kitchen Raanaa took a broom to him and shooed him out the door. The thought of making a threatening gesture toward a tiger would normally have paralyzed a villager, but Sarang had the uncanny ability to make people forget what he was.

There are problems inherent in keeping a tiger in a house, even in a jungle village. The problem that caused constant concern was his diet. Sarang may not have acted very much like a tiger but he had a tiger's appetite. He retained his fondness for milk and rice gruel, but meat was his staple and meat he had to have. Several fishermen in the village were co-operative and there was a steady supply of small river fish which Sarang accepted as a meat substitute. Ata took to hunting in the nearby forest and a regular supply of small game took care of the balance of his needs. There was no thought of turning him loose to hunt. In fact, he was loose and could come and go as he pleased. He was often seen walking between Satwyne's hut and the hunting lodge and most of the villagers paid him little attention.

Some of Sarang's habits were inherently unpleasant and there were days when his presence in the lodge was anything but a joy, particularly for Liz. It was impossible to housebreak him, and his urine contained a high percentage of ammonia. He had favorite spots and unless he was caught heading for them and driven outdoors in time the house would smell for hours. The boys became less enchanted as time went on and they found themselves boiling water and scrubbing the badly bleached floor several times a day. The one time that he chose the middle of Liz's bed for his toilet caused a near revolution and Sarang was banned from her bedroom ever after.

Sarang shed as well, and here again it meant extra work for the houseboys, but it wasn't as bad as his less than considerate toilet habits. The one single habit that upset Liz most was Sarang's attention to his claws. Although he never displayed any of his eighteen scimitars to his friends, no piece of furniture was safe from the ten on his front paws. Left alone for any length of time he could all but destroy every scrap of fabric in the room. It wasn't that he was purposely destructive, it was just that he obviously derived great pleasure from hooking his claws into a soft, fibrous material and feeling the tug as he pulled downward. Rattan furniture was almost as good, and several chairs and a settee eventually had to be consigned to the bonfire. One day, after Sarang had shredded a woven mat partition between two rooms, Liz went into a tirade listing all of the cub's faults. She topped the list with a spluttering insult: "And . . . and he even has bad breath!"

Pamela looked at her mother with hurt eyes. "But Mummy, you don't have to kiss him if you don't want to."

There were other discussions regarding Sarang to

be heard in Pukmaranpur. There were villagers who were not involved with the stench of his urine, his destructive habits or his shedding hair. They were men who would never get close enough to know whether Sarang had bad breath or not.

"They have made *baghh* forget who he is but one day he will remember." It was said often and the seed of serious trouble lay in those words.

The more moderate of his detractors wanted him removed from the village and turned loose. The more pessimistic felt that he knew too much about the ways of man ever to be safe and that he would have to be destroyed.

The most remarkable part of the relationship between Khoka and the tiger began accidentally and developed quite as a matter of course. Because Khoka liked physical contact he moved about with his hand touching some part of Sarang's body. Generally, because of Sarang's habit of pressing against the legs of anyone he especially liked, Khoka's hand rested on the tiger's shoulders, just back of his neck. In time they developed the habit of walking that way and Khoka began moving about with some of the freedom he had had with Prince. Liz saw them walking down a path that way one day and happened to mention it at dinner that night. Pamela had never thought of it in quite those terms and Liz's observation sparked the idea. The next morning, with the co-operation of the ever-helpful Raanaa, Prince's har-

ness was duplicated from available materials and Sarang was fitted out to become unofficially the world's
first Seeing Eye tiger.

Even some of his critics had to admit that there
was something special about this *baghh* as he led the
blind boy across the plaza for the first time. But
they were the moderates. The more outspoken of his
enemies only shook their heads. "It is just one more
trick to make *baghh* forget what surely he will one
day remember."

In fact there was some justification for the fears
these people expressed. While there are few tigers
left in the Chittagong Hill Tracts, East Pakistan in-
cludes another remote area known as the Sunderbans.
The Sunderbans are reputed to have had more man-
eating tigers than any other comparable land area
and the infamy of those dreaded cats has spread far
and wide. With good reason the jungle peoples of the
country have a tradition of fearing *baghh*. Eventually
the private rumblings reached the ears of the village
elders and Manik and Masu brought their misgivings
to Glenn.

They explained that they had tried discussing it
with Satwyne but had gotten nowhere. The *phandi,*
a fiercely independent man, had threatened to walk
his elephant through the hut of the first person to
raise a hand against the cat. He would not have his
boy hurt again. Satwyne's temper and his physical
strength were not unknown quantities and Masu and

Manik retreated to the hunting lodge in the hopes of finding a more reasonable attitude.

Glenn dreaded this conversation, although he had known for a long time that it was coming. He didn't have an answer and had been unable to devise any point of view that could lead to one. He ducked the issue by pointing out that the cat belonged to Satwyne and not to him, for it had been Satwyne who had brought it home to Khoka. He stood on the veranda watching Manik and Masu walk down the trail past Pamela and Khoka, who were coming up toward the lodge, Sarang leading the boy just as Prince had done. As he stood there he knew the issue was only temporarily put aside. It was plain, too, that the elders knew it as well. This was the first encounter and they had been polite. But the pressure was on them and they would be back. He dreaded the decision that one day he knew would have to be made.

12

The Trio

The logistics of feeding even a small herd of working elephants can be a staggering problem, Glenn was to learn. Despite their huge size they are not particularly hardy animals and when maintained in captivity great care must be taken to see that they get the food they need. Each of his captives required one hundred and seventy pounds of dry fodder in addition to four hundred pounds of fresh cut greens each day, for the elephant's digestive system is one of the least economical in the world. Along with the mountains of fodder it was necessary to supply them with a food concentrate of rice, coarse flour, *gur* (a kind of native molasses), cooked onions, and tamarind pulp. The mixture was rolled into balls and enriched with salt and ground nut oil. Much less than a hundred grams of salt a day per animal would have endangered their health while they were working. Together they produced two hundred and sixty pounds of solid waste matter that had to be disposed of every twenty-four hours. To Glenn it seemed that an elephant was a creature designed by God to whom you brought one mountain and away from whom you carted another. It was only logical that a private joke around the lodge should evolve from this observation. The captive elephants became known as the mountaineers.

Water supply continued to be a problem. Each elephant needed a minimum of one hundred and ninety quarts every day. Each of them could consume seventy quarts in one session. Glenn watched the carriers bringing the water up from the river and remembered with fondness the lovely, choking, greasy smell of diesel fuel and exhaust. Even he saw the irony in his fond memories of farm machinery.

The time would come, of course, when the new elephants could be taken to the river and watered there. Eventually they could be released in the nearby forest to browse all night and be collected again in the morning. For a period of many weeks, though, cutters went out in teams to haul back enormous loads of fodder from *peepal* and banyan trees, along with the *ficus*, jack and bamboo greens, palm tops, *neem* leaves, sugar cane, and the leaves and stems of plantain trees. Jackfruits, melons, pineapples, *palmyara* or fan palm, coconut meat and other wild fruits rounded out the complicated diet. It seemed to Glenn that maintaining the elephants was a full time occupation that would leave little opportunity for working them. In time, though, it all began to fit together as a routine and the supply problems seemed less overwhelming.

Shortly after the captives had entered into the one-*koonki* stage of their training the beautiful Begam Bahar fell ill. She seemed perfectly healthy one day and was seriously distressed the next. The first sign she gave of impending trouble was the languor of her movement. Elephants are constant movers. They weave, rock, flick their ears, swish their trunks, are seldom still unless really sick. Soon Begam Bahar was not moving at all. She refused food, even her favorite fresh-cut pineapples that were normally given to her only as a reward for good behavior. Her eyes were reddened and a yellow discharge stained her cheeks. Although there was no thermometer available that was up to the task it was apparent that she was running a temperature. Glenn despaired for her life. The thought of losing her made him frantic to act, to do something, anything, to save her, and a conference was called to which Oroon, Satwyne, Ata, Manik and Masu came. Since it was not the rainy season and since they could detect no bleeding from her mucous membranes they ruled out the dreaded anthrax. Still, she was suffering from some kind of infection or disability and there was reason enough for genuine concern. Although no diagnosis was possible it was apparent that certain precautions had to be taken without delay.

As a first step they removed Sikander from the area. Elephants, Ata explained, are extremely susceptible to infection and whatever was bothering Begam Bahar would be likely to infect the *makhna* as well. Next, all fodder and dung in the *pilkhana* area was raked together and burned. New water buckets were brought in for both elephants and the old ones were buried. The amount of fresh water available to the sick cow was doubled and all dry fodder eliminated. Her green fodder, now her exclusive bulk food, was not mixed but kept in separate piles so that she could choose what she wanted. None of her feed was brought in from swampy areas and a huge lean-to was erected to shield her from the sun. Young boys stayed with her constantly, brushing away any flies that came near.

The crisis seemed to come on the second day when she sank to her knees and rolled over on her left hindquarter. Glenn was certain it was the end, and half made up his mind to put her out of her misery. He decided to give her another hour. The sight of so magnificent an animal made helpless was almost more than he could bear. She held her jaws open and made deep rumbling and sighing sounds. For about fifteen minutes she struggled but seemed unable to rise. Then, slowly, she managed to right herself. She hesitated, then drank deeply from the buckets of clear water that were kept nearby and after about an hour sampled some sugar cane. Glenn nearly wept with joy as it became apparent that the crisis had passed.

Because an elephant's vital processes are slow, an infection generally runs a protracted course. It was a week before the beautiful cow began to show some signs of her former spirit, and her training was deferred for ten days. At the end of that period it was obvious that the disease had burned itself out and that Begam Bahar would survive. The area was spread to a depth of two feet with dry straw which was set on fire. Only after it had been thoroughly raked and the ashes buried was Sikander moved back and the normal routine reinstated.

Several weeks after the crisis with Begam Bahar, Ma and Kala, who had been elevated to the role of *mahout*, began taking the two trainees to the river in the afternoon. On order the elephants were taught to lie down in water just deep enough to cover their bodies. Periodically the tips of their trunks would emerge like snorkels, enabling them to breathe. The *mahouts* scrubbed them with freshly cut coconut husks, a process that took two hours each day. The elephants seemed to enjoy the treatment and responded well to the pleasurable contact with their masters. They were worked for three hours early every morning and three hours again late in the afternoon. Between ten in the morning and three o'clock in the afternoon they were tethered to heavy logs in the forest and allowed to browse. Surprisingly for such large animals, elephants have a delicate constitution and lack any great powers of endurance. They are not bothered by rain but are subject to sun stroke and cannot tolerate cold winds. By having their activities carefully scheduled, they can be called upon to do extremely heavy labor — but only for six hours a day, only when properly fed and watered, and only when permitted to escape the heat of midday in deep shade. All of this Glenn learned, and all of this information was applied in laying out the experimental schedule designed to convert wild jungle animals into agricultural beasts of burden. With the exception of Begam Bahar's sudden illness everything was going according to schedule.

The world for the two children centered on Sarang. His temperament remained constant despite his rapid growth and although he was large enough to cause serious injury he exhibited no inclination to misuse his powers. He took endless roughing up and even carried the children on his back. He seemed to sense Khoka's disability and was particularly gentle with him. He seemed to understand as well that Khoka could not come directly to him as Pamela could and when he saw the boy stretch his hands out in front of him he would move in and brush against his legs. Khoka would inevitably fall to his knees and hug the great cat around the neck, burying his face in his fur. Sarang would stand firm and purr, his purr being almost the equivalent of a roar in a lesser animal. At times he would turn and rake the boy's face with his rasp-like tongue. Khoka never noticed his breath.

When the children played too roughly he would terminate the game by pinning them to the ground with his forepaws. His claws never showed except when he sharpened them on a tree or Liz's favorite chair or stretched them out in accompaniment to one of his mighty yawns, but the force he could exert downward could pin either child. When he had them immobilized he generally took the opportunity to rasp their faces and leave them giggling and soaked with drool. He was responsive to their commands and would come bounding to their sides when they called him. On occasion he would knock Pamela off her feet by bumping against her but he never did it to Khoka. When the crude harness that Raanaa had fashioned for him was strapped across his chest he led Khoka slowly, not unlike the way Prince had done. There was a running discussion around the lodge as to whether or not Sarang really understood. The children, of course, favored the theory that he did.

The hunting lodge with its great sprawling complex of rooms became a second home for Khoka. Several nights each week he would curl up with Sarang on a pile of woven mats and sleep content in the knowledge that Pamela was in the next room. His English had improved steadily and both Liz and Glenn were able to communicate with him. In time they came to think of him as a second child and Liz secretly dreaded the day when they would have to leave him behind. Glenn saw in Liz's growing fondness for the boy the early stages of a fixation. He worried, but knew there was nothing he could do to prevent it from running its course.

The rules that were established after Prince's death were very firm. Neither child was permitted on any forest trail and they could cross over into the outlying paddy fields only when adults were in sight. Once the initial terror passed Liz stopped checking their whereabouts every hour but the basic rules remained the same. Glenn's encounter with the king cobra had sharpened their awareness of the potential danger from that quarter and Pamela received a number of lectures on alertness and caution, even within the village itself. Even though the king cobra was unlikely to approach a human settlement, the lesser common cobras appeared fairly regularly on rat hunts and were a constant menace, especially toward dusk when the heat of the day was past. Despite all the restrictions, however, there were still enough new worlds to conquer, and the now familiar trio of boy, girl and tiger were seen in every quarter of the village and in the immediately surrounding agricultural areas.

Some of the fields surrounding the village were far enough removed from the center of activity to allow wildlife from the adjacent forest lands to intrude. In their wanderings the trio often encountered smaller animals but strangely enough Sarang showed no inclination to attack.

Khoka saw the animals only through Pamela's eyes and much of their conversation centered on her descriptions and his recall of the legends he had heard. *Sial* the fox was encountered fairly often, although Pamela rarely caught more than a fleeting glimpse of him. Khoka spoke of the little canine's wisdom and of his skill in outwitting animals with greater strength. Once when Sarang drew back with a snarl, the first they had heard him issue since his earliest days with them, an eight-foot python slithered across an open spot between two clumps of brush. It was brown all over with prominent dark gray-edged rhomboid marks down its back. It had recently shed and its skin was iridescent in the brilliant sun. Pamela excitedly described the great snake to Khoka, who warned her of the dangers the mighty *aujaugor* presented to the unwary. In fact Khoka possessed an amazing knowledge of the world around him. He had always been a good listener, not easily distracted as sighted children are, and he had a particularly retentive memory. Occasionally he found some difficulty in trying to link Pamela's description with the native name he knew. Once he was able to make an association, though, the character of the creature came to mind. He spoke of *shaujaroo* the porcupine, *pancha* the owl, whose evening call he could recognize, and of *bedji* the swift mongoose, who was the friend of man even though it killed his chickens under his hut. Pamela was a little bothered by the fact that Khoka's knowledge was often based on legend and superstition and not on anything observable about the animal itself. She chided him and urged him to be more "scientific." Each time she did he would ask her what the word meant and she would be at a loss to explain it. She eventually came to the conclusion that this was one bridge she was unable to construct.

The children had reason enough to fear another encounter with *baghh*, although their love for Sarang had done much to ease their memory of the experience they had had on the dark forest trail. Neither of them thought of Sarang as the cub of the tigress that killed Prince, although they knew it to be true. Somehow, Sarang transcended such ordinary associations and belonged to neither the village nor the forest. He was apart, a special creature, a very special strength. This was even more profoundly so for Khoka than for Pamela, for his cultural heritage was far richer than hers in special creatures, special powers, and the need for both.

Of all the big cats the tiger is perhaps the least excitable. He has a particular calm about him, an easy way of going about things that has made him an object of respect except in areas where one has gone bad and taken to hunting men. Sarang could be characterized by this quality of calm perhaps more than by any other. As he grew he became more and more a veritable mountain of a cat, solid, immovable except when it suited his fancy, and placid. He would sit for hours or walk for miles, whatever the children wanted to do. At times, though, when he felt really stubborn, nothing they could do would get him to move. He was not perturbed by the dogs that yapped at his passage nor attracted by the chickens that scurried out of his way as they moved down the trails near the small clusters of huts. There was a regal quality in his calm, and a reassurance. Not since his very first hours in their charge had they seen him exhibit any temper and it seemed impossible that he could ever represent a threat of any kind.

It was all the more surprising to them, then, when one day Sarang suddenly sprang clear of Khoka's grasp with an explosive snarl and stood a few feet off with his lip rolled back. They had been walking along a familiar path that led to an enormous banyan tree where they often went to sit in the heat of the day. He stood quartering away from them, his tail lashing, a volcanic rumbling deep in his throat. Khoka had been thrown to the ground by the sudden movement and Pamela huddled near where he lay sprawled in the path. She stared at Sarang as he slowly inched forward, his eyes fixed, his teeth bared. When he was about six feet away he dropped to his stomach, wiggled his hindquarters for better purchase and launched forward like an enormous spring. He passed clear over their heads and crashed into the brush on the far side of the trail. A roar erupted as he landed, answered by another.

The children had neither seen nor heard the other half-grown tiger that had moved in behind them, and although it did not represent a threat to them, Sarang's reaction had been violent and instantaneous. Pamela saw the other tiger for just an instant. Sarang's claws were fastened into its flanks as it struggled to get free. It turned and slashed out but Sarang was the quicker and escaped injury. The intruder turned to flee but Sarang was on him again. Their battle carried them behind the screen of thick brushes and all the children could tell of its progress were the screams and roars of rage that sent every bird in the area into the sky calling its alarm notes. It was soon over. The second tiger broke free and made for the forest, trailing blood from its severely lacerated hindquarters.

It soon found its mother and came limping to her side. If Sarang had encountered this other young male when its mother was close at hand he would not have survived. Fortunately, he met him after he had wandered off from the hollow where the female was bedded down.

The noise of the fracas had carried back to the village and by the time Sarang emerged from the bushes several adults were hovering over the two children. They backed off as Sarang approached, not certain that it was Sarang at all. Pamela knew immediately and ran forward and threw her arms around his neck. He was still tense from the encounter and relaxed only after Pamela spoke softly to him and scratched him under the chin, his most vulnerable spot. He stopped lashing his tail and slowly sat down in the pathway. Khoka inched forward on his hands and knees until he was up against the great cat. For Khoka, touch was the reassuring sense. The adults stood looking at them for a long moment and then turned back to the village. Although Sarang had in fact acted as the children's protector, he had reminded the villagers of something most of them had all but forgotten: Sarang would in time be a full-grown tiger, a large male, with enormous power and the ability to unleash savage energy. The fact that his staggering potential had been unleashed in defense of the children on this one occasion did not assure its direction the next time it was summoned up. Those who spoke out against him, in fact, were prepared to forgive him for anything, except for being a tiger.

There was a meeting in Pukmaranpur that night and several people who had heard the battle and seen Sarang at his savage best rose to speak. Before the meeting was over, Raanaa, who loved the little cub almost as much as the children did, had slipped away and brought the news to the lodge. Pamela and Khoka were in the next room, pressed against the thin partition, as Raanaa described the rising temper of the villagers. It was then that they vowed to each other that if Sarang were ever driven from Pukmaranpur they would go with him. Fate had taken Prince from them but no power on earth would take away their beloved tiger.

13

The Legend

Later, looking back on it, Glenn would be unable to find any sense in his actions, for they had been doomed from the first to amount to nothing. Perhaps, he would later muse, there was some faint hope in the back of my mind that if the whole thing could be made less conspicuous the problem would fade away.

Quite simply, once he saw the inevitable pressure mounting toward an equally inevitable conclusion, he began to restrict the movements of his daughter, and therefore of Khoka and Sarang, for the three were inseparable.

As a first exercise of authority over their freedom the children were told that Sarang must never again be walked through the village proper or near the market or, for that matter, near any place where people gathered together. Through Ata, Glenn obtained Satwyne's agreement to have Khoka and Sarang moved into the lodge full-time, thus removing Sarang from the center of the village where he was most conspicuous. This first move didn't bother the children because it enabled Khoka to spend all of his time with Pamela. He had also become extremely fond of Liz. It was a natural enough attraction for a child who had been without a mother for most of his life. Needs and longings within him that he had repressed in self-defense came to light, and more and more he wanted to be with the compact family and to have access to the mother figure at its center. Liz, Glenn's eternal Earth-Mother, responded in kind and became increasingly disturbed by the thought of losing Khoka when it came time for them to leave Pukmaranpur. She found herself in a strangely reversed emotional bind and the day she had once looked forward to with almost pathological longing came to hold little but dread for her. She tore down the calendar on which she had been ticking off the days and tried pushing the separation out of her mind altogether.

Very shortly after the symbol of Liz's homesickness vanished from the wall Glenn noticed its absence and knew immediately what was on his wife's mind. In fact, he had predicted it. He knew that they would have to talk it out sooner or later and his opening shot was experimental. They were standing alone on the veranda absorbing the jungle night. The soft, interrogative *wut? wut? wut?* of a scops owl drifted down to them from the edge of the forest followed by the little bird's bubbly chattering note.

"I love that sound, Glenn. It's kind of sad and lonely yet it always seems to end on a note of hope."

"You're going to miss this place, aren't you? In spite of everything."

"Some parts of it, yes, I am."

Liz sighed meaningfully and Glenn let a five-beat pause slip by.

"Like Khoka?"

"Glenn! Let's take him home with us. We can give him everything, every chance he can never have here. Please, let's take him away with us."

"Honey, he isn't some kind of pet we can pick up and just take along. He's got a family here, at least a father, and a religion we don't know anything about, and traditions. It's not all that easy."

"I don't care whether it's easy or not. All I want to know is — is it possible? Because if it's possible then we can do it. Satwyne's no fool. He'll want what's best for his son. He'll know we can get him treatment and care he could never get here, not in another five generations."

Liz turned to her husband and looked up into his face. Her eyes were pleading, reaching out to him.

"Honey, I don't even know what it is I'm agreeing to. I guess if you're asking me if I'll agree to adopt Khoka, all other things being equal — whatever the hell that means — okay, if you want to, okay. We certainly won't get an argument from Pamela!"

Liz hugged him tightly and the enormity of what he had just said swept over him. My God, he thought, I've just agreed to raise another man's child as my own son, a blind child at that, with a Seeing Eye tiger — a Buddhist with dark skin in white Wichita!

There was no point in recounting his misgivings to his wife. He knew full well that if she had been the kind of person who would have accepted them she wouldn't have been the girl he had wanted so desperately to marry and whom he had loved so fully all these years.

They agreed to say nothing of the adoption idea until they knew more about it. Would Khoka want to leave the security of his own people, speaking his own language, for the unknown? Would Satwyne ever agree to the idea? What were the regulations laid down by the United States government, and what were the rules of adoption in Pakistan? They agreed that they were a long way from a workable solution. Better to say nothing for the time being.

The stormy meeting that had taken place in Puk-maranpur after Sarang's brave but terrifying skirmish had far-reaching effects. Quite inexplicably a Bengali copy of *Man-Eaters of Sunderbans* by Tahawar Ali Khan began making the rounds. There were enough people who could read it to themselves and to their neighbors so that its contents could become general knowledge. Several weeks after it appeared Manik managed to get hold of it and bring it to the lodge. Sitting in front of a sizzling lantern on the veranda after dinner Ata translated for Glenn:

Of course, the enterprising fisherman or wood-cutter has to penetrate deep into the forest, but he knows that his exploit may one day end in a horrible death. Once, when I was camping in a launch, I heard that the night before a tiger had carried off in one leap one of the three men who had anchored their small boat in the middle of a 20 foot wide creek. And only a few weeks ago, a man was dragged . . .

"Okay Ata, thanks. I have the picture. This anti-Sarang clique must have hired a PR firm to help them out!"

Each day a new complaint came in and the areas where the children could go with Sarang became fewer and fewer. Sarang frightened a man's bullock, who ran off, shattering the man's plow on a rock. Sarang frightened a man's extremely elderly mother and made her fall down an embankment. A man was missing two chickens where Sarang was known to have been that same morning.

Glenn could sense the mounting determination of what had become known around the lodge as "The Opposition." He began to sense as well that since the hunting lodge was the center of the elephant experiment and also now officially the tiger's home the one might start affecting the other. The one thing he knew could doom the entire experiment was happening before his eyes. He was emerging as a figure running against the mainstream of village consensus.

He had been waiting for two days to get Manik and Masu alone. He felt his proposal was the one chance he had to find a compromise.

"Do you think the villagers will be satisfied if we build a cage and lock Sarang up?"

The elders nodded. Yes, they believed this would satisfy almost everyone. But the cage would have to be strong, strong enough to hold a wild tiger, and not be just a pen for a household pet.

Glenn shrank from the job that faced him that night, but it had to be done. The days when the three could wander together were over. Sarang would have to leave forever, be caged, or done away with. There were no other choices. There were no tears, no pleas, just the quiet reasoning voice of an intelligent little girl looking up at her father. Khoka and Pamela were sitting on the floor with Sarang sprawled out between them. Sarang was sucking on Khoda's rolled up fist.

"Daddy, do you think Sarang deserves to be locked up in a cage? Why are you against him now? What has he done that's wrong?"

Glenn could hear Liz leave the room behind him. He felt himself at a loss for words; Pamela was not old enough to think her father incapable of righting a wrong. He wanted to rant, rave, smash things, anything but cope with the questions that were now inevitable.

"Honey, I don't think that Sarang has done anything wrong. That's not the point at all."

"Then why do you want to put him in a jail?"

It's not a jail. It's a way of protecting him from people who don't like him and to protect everybody from the harm he *might* do to them *someday*."

He knew he wasn't doing too well: mainly, he had to admit, because he didn't believe in what he was saying. He was begging out of a fight, for the sake of his experiment. Worst of all, Pamela realized it, and was bewildered. She had heard him speak so often of the importance of sticking up for what you believe in your heart to be right, no matter what other people say.

He looked down into his daughter's earnest, inquiring face and in desperation resorted to the oldest weapon of all, the parental ultimatum.

"Pamela, I'm sorry you can't seem to understand it, I really am, but this is the way it *has* to be."

But, like all retreating armies, he left himself vulnerable to attack from the rear.

"Oh, but Daddy, I do understand. Truly I do. It's just that sometimes it's very hard for kids to know which one of their father's faces to believe."

Glenn was too stunned to answer and before he could bring his dismay under control Pamela, Khoka and Sarang were out of the room.

Liz was still awake when Glenn, somewhat subdued, pushed aside the curtain and came into their bedroom. He had been out walking — and thinking.

"Are you awake, honey?"

She lay very still, having half made up her mind to avoid the issue for the night. She was aware, though, of the utter unfairness of doing so and relented.

"I've been waiting for you. I figured that you'd want to talk."

"How the devil am I going to make her understand? I know she thinks I've let her down and I don't want her to think that. On the other hand I can't fight city hall, which is just about what we have been doing."

"Leave it to me. I'll talk to her in the morning."

She could hear Glenn undressing and climbing into his bed a few feet away from her own. She sighed, "God, how I hate twin beds!"

She listened for a moment and heard him get up

again. The sound the cot made as it was shoved across the floor was rasping and loud in the quiet lodge. In the distance a night bird cackled, listened for its own echo, and cackled again.

"Paamela, do you know about the *Shadhoobaba?*"

Although it was an unmistakable infraction of the rules for Pamela to leave her room once she had been put to bed, she had wanted to be with both Khoka and Sarang and was just rebellious enough tonight to disobey. She sat cross-legged on the floor next to Khoka's mat stroking Sarang, who lay stretched out next to the boy. She had heard Khoka refer to the *Shadhoobaba* several times earlier in their linguistic exercises but it wasn't clear in her mind what he meant by it.

"No, Khoka, I don't. What is it?"

"It is a man who can see in front of him and know what will come. He lives alone and can talk with all the *janoar*. He is very wise."

Pamela had heard of a legendary hermit who could talk with the animals of the jungle but hadn't associated him with the term *Shadhoobaba*.

"Does he really know the future?"

"*Hae.* The animals tell him what they see and what they have learned. He knows everything that men know and everything the animals know. He is very wise."

Although Khoka's disability made him dependent

on Pamela in many ways and could make it appear that she was the dominant personality, quite the opposite was true. In Wichita, surrounded by telephones, automobiles and washing machines, he might have slipped into a follower's role, but in Pukmaranpur, where Pamela was untutored in the legends, languages, and traditions, he was her guide. In their hours of conversation she listened to him as he explained things to her with great patience.

"Do you know the *Shadhoobaba?*"

"*Na.* No one can know him. He never comes to people, but some people can go to him and he will tell them what is to come."

Khoka hummed softly to himself, something he often did when overcome by a sense of profound wonder.

"He is very, very wise. He is the wisest man in the world, for what he doesn't know he can ask the *cil* in the sky, the fish in the river, even the *koomeer* who has lived a thousand years, and *hati* the elephant who never forgets. A man once told me that the *Shadhoobaba* can even talk to the rocks and the trees but I don't know if he can. It is also said that he can close his eyes and be anywhere."

Pamela was intrigued not only because a good story was in the offing but also because it had occurred to her, just as it obviously had to Khoka, that there might be a connection between their present plight and a man so wise that he knew everything.

"Where does he live?"

"In the forest."

"Do you know where?"

"Sarang does. All the animals do. He lives in a place where the people have gone. There is a great temple that is hidden by the forest. The *purano lokera* — the last people — built it and then went away to another world to be nearer to their gods. The *mondir* remains and it is guarded by the *Shadhoobaba's* friends the *janoar*."

Pamela had heard of the ancient temples built thousands of years ago by people who had disappeared and in fact, on the day Sarang's mother killed Prince, she had been looking for a ruined edifice that was erroneously reputed to be just outside of Pukmaranpur.

"Can people see the *Shadhoobaba?* Will the animals let them into the temple?"

"The *Shadhoobaba* looks through the stone walls of the *mondir* and decides if the people are worthy. If he thinks *Hae!* the *janoar* knows his thoughts and the people are not injured. If the *Shadhoobaba* thinks *Na!* the people are killed."

"How does one become worthy?"

"Only the *Shadhoobaba* knows that."

Pamela sat thinking for a long time. The image of the ancient meditative hermit sitting in a jungle-shrouded temple protected by a phalanx of wild animals was an intriguing one. It might have been an

interesting if somewhat fanciful story had she heard
it in Wichita. Sitting on a woven reed mat only yards
from the jungle with her hand resting on the flank
of a tiger made it something else again. The *wut?*
wut? wut? of the scops owl was a confirming force
in the environment. She was very receptive, the more
so perhaps because the story was coming as privileged information from her own peer, and she was
still feeling emotionally estranged from her father.

"Paamela?"

Pamela came to with a start. She had been dozing,
with the image of the *Shadhoobaba* floating before
her.

"What, Khoka?"

"The *Shadhoobaba* could tell me about my eyes,
too. Sarang could take us there. He knows the way."

Pamela knew that what they were planning was
wrong and frighteningly dangerous. She knew it but
there was an inexorableness about the situation and
she yielded to it. Sarang had been sent to them, just
as she had been sent to Khoka. Through no fault of
her own, without her consent or will, she had been
transported from the white frame house at the corner of Irving Place and Massey Avenue in the middle
of the United States of America to Pukmaranpur in
the middle of an Asian jungle. She had been given a
blind native boy as a guide into the mysteries of the
East and a partially grown tiger as a plaything. She
had been put into this highly unlikely situation and

been told about the meditative hermit who could answer all questions and solve all problems. She had even been given problems that no one, not even her own father, seemed able to solve. It had to be with a purpose or none of it made any sense at all. It was all entirely too unlikely to have happened otherwise. Her Protestant upbringing had given her a solid connection with the concept of fate, so although she felt that what she was doing was cruel to her parents, it was inevitable and she was sure they would understand.

A tiger's passage is not something you are apt to hear, even if you are listening for it. Two barefoot children walking on the balls of their feet can be almost as silent. No one heard them leave the lodge at two in the morning and no one saw them pass through the towering black screen that marked the boundary between the village of Pukmaranpur and the vast jungle that spread ahead of them across the remaining territory of East Pakistan, across the southward projecting finger of the Indian state of Assam, across Burma to southern China and the Indo-Chinese Peninsula. Before them lay millions upon millions of acres of jungle, and although much of it has been occupied by men and their antecedents for thousands of generations, much of it is yet to be explored. Pamela, Khoka and Sarang were drawn into that jungle by a magnet that has manipulated the philosophies of the East for as long as there have been men there to create them. The magnet was the belief that somewhere behind the curtain of the unknown, as symbolized so often by the jungle, somewhere beyond the boundaries of human experience, there was a force that could answer the questions the human brain was evolved just far enough to pose, but not far enough to answer. Pamela and Khoka called it *Shadhoobaba*, but men have been following it for thousands of years, calling it by hundreds of different names.

14

The Jungle

Since men first began recording their thoughts they have written of the jungle as a place that "swallows" people up. It is no accident that this analogy has lasted so long or has been so often repeated. The jungle — the warm, green, wet, dark and instantly regenerative jungle — is like the sea in that it will open only briefly at its periphery to allow an invasion. It soon closes its own wound, leaving only a few ripples to show that there has been an intrusion. Once a person perforates the wall he belongs to the jungle, he is a part of it, and although he may pass through it without harm, he is subject to the forces that have kept it intact for millions of years. The intruder is in his turn humbled by that which he has come to conquer.

The sun was four hours away to the east when Pamela, Khoka and Sarang passed through the wall to lose themselves in the jungle. The children were aliens, for it had been thousands of years since Khoka's forbears had emerged from under the canopy to live instead along its edges and Pamela's antecedents from Northern Europe had never known such a place at all. Sarang alone belonged, although even his heritage was of quite a different world. He was not the descendent of original jungle cats like *chita baghh* the leopard, for his kind had come south thousands of years before from Siberia, Korea, and northern China. Still, the tigers from which he had come had been in tropical Asia long enough for it to have become part of them and they part of it. Sarang was at home. Although the random stripes that marked his tawny coat had been designed by nature to hide the hunter in the summer grasses of northern marshes, he blended here as well.

Their passage was almost silent. The open floor between the trees was matted with soft debris that cushioned their steps. Each acre of the jungle received several tons of animal and vegetable matter every year, matter that rained down to disintegrate there and feed the towering trees.

Although there were places where smaller plants crowded together to form all but impassable tangles near surface water, most of the forest was open and flat, almost like a cathedral, and they penetrated with ease into its deeper places. By dawn they would have to have made their way deep into the forest. Pursuit was certain and recovery sure unless they were far enough away to frustrate their trackers.

They moved swiftly, quietly, allowing Sarang to lead them. He moved with an easy grace and the children huddled against his sides so as not to lose him in the darkness. They could feel the muscles rippling under his coat and his strength and sureness became theirs in part. Khoka clung to the harness and Pamela rested a hand on Sarang's back for reassurance. Twice she felt a wave of terror start down deep and begin swelling within her, and twice she swallowed it back. It was not an easy thing for a little girl to do.

Sarang stopped suddenly and stood rigid, listening, his head stiffly alert, his ears moving slightly. Nearby, a tall tangle of ferns, of a kind older than the flowering plants by millions of years, stood like severe feathery sentinals. There was no movement, no sound the children could detect, but Sarang had been alerted and refused to move. The children felt his tension and it occurred to them simultaneously how very helpless they were without him. Khoka gripped the harness tighter and Pamela pushed her leg harder against the tiger's flank.

The ten-foot python that lay coiled at the foot of the fern tangle, digesting the young boar it had taken thirty hours earlier, knew of the children's approach. Although deaf, its contact with the forest floor was intimate and sensitive. It felt them coming and flicked its forked tongue in and out, snatching up small samples of air to take back into its mouth, there to test them for telltale particles of odor. It is doubtful that it would have bothered the children unless they had stumbled close enough to frighten it, but Sarang was alerted and would not permit them to pass near the ferns. Without ever knowing that the giant reptile was there the children were forced to move around it in a wide circle.

Even if you are an adult who can control his fancies the jungle at noon can be an eerie place. For two small children the jungle a few hours before dawn is terrifying. Although silent when compared with a city street or a village square it is of course a place of a million sounds, most of them too soft to permit recognition. It is the fact that they are all but impossible to identify that makes them so ominous.

The jungle, like every other place, has its twenty-four-hour feeders, animals whose metabolism is so rapid that they must eat around the clock or starve to death. While the python beneath the ferns might not eat again for two or even three weeks, the shrews whose passage across the floor whispered and hissed at the children could be dead seven hours after a hardy meal if denied the opportunity to feed again. Beetles almost the size of Khoka's clenched fist rustled the rotting leaves as they moved and cockroaches the size of Pamela's thumb made an audible plop as they fell from nearby bushes to the forest floor. Night frogs shrilled occasionally, and lizards disturbed in their rest scurried to escape, sounding very much like snakes as they burrowed under the carpet of rotting fruit, decaying fronds, animal droppings, and the empty hulls of insects that had been drained of life and discarded by the tiny cannibals of the forest floor.

Neither child knew the direction of their travel and they followed Sarang, trusting in him to bring them to the ruined temple that was the home of the fabled *Shadhoobaba*. For Sarang it was just another walk like so many others they had taken. As much a creature of the night as the day he was unable to make any distinction between this outing and the dozens of others he had gone on with them. It was all the same to him, for now as in the past he had no place to go, no place he would rather be than with his two young friends.

When the first faint streaks of light began slipping through the canopy from the east the children were six miles north of Pukmaranpur. They had come to a small stream that meandered across the forest floor seeking the Gamalbuk River and eventually Lake Karnaphuli. The water they drank from cupped hands was less than an hour away from the village. The fruit bats stirring amid the leaves of the fig tree overhead paid little heed to the strange sight below: a tiger, a native boy, and a small white girl huddled side by side at the edge of the stream drinking from the cool sweet water that bubbled up out of the ground only a few dozen yards off.

"Khoka. *Klanto achi*."

And Pamela *was* tired. It was the first time in her eleven years she had gone through an entire night without sleep. Their long hike and the tension that naturally gripped them during their nighttime flight through the jungle had taken their toll.

"*Hae*. I am tired, too, Paamela. But not so much."

"I'll bet Sarang is tired."

"*Na*. My father told me the *baghh* is never tired when he has something to do. That is why he rests all the time when he has nothing to do."

"Let's rest here, Khoka. Just a little while."

"Okay. If you are tired, Paamela, we can rest."

Pamela smoothed out some leaves beside a thick banyan tree and the two children nestled down with Sarang between them. Khoka was the first to fall asleep and for some minutes Pamela rested her head on Sarang's shoulder, watching the blind boy. The early sun was just brushing his features with a soft ray of light that had found its way down through the tangle overhead. As she was falling off to sleep the happy thought occurred to her that when she awoke it would all prove to have been nothing but a bad dream, and that her mother would be standing next to her bed, as she had been nearly every morning since the day Pamela was born.

Liz read the note for the twentieth time. Pamela's handwriting was not particularly good under ideal conditions and it had worsened considerably under the stress of writing in extreme haste in almost total darkness.

Dear Mummy and Daddy,

Please don't worry. We will be back very soon. We have gone to see the Shadhoobaba about Khoka's eyes and the problem with Sarang.

Love X X X X X

Pamela

Liz was through crying. She was numb, she was angry and she was frightened. She could hardly believe that Pamela would have run away or could have been foolish enough to enter the jungle at night. She held the note in her lap, her two hands crushing its edges, and stared straight ahead. Time and again the picture Pamela had given her of the tigress's sudden attack on Prince flashed across her mind. She couldn't cry anymore. She could hardly think.

"How many of these damned hermits are there, Ata?"

"Glenn, there are hundreds of them, maybe thousands of them. They're scattered all across Asia."

Ata explained again, slowly, although he didn't expect Glenn to grasp what he was saying. He had been trying to explain since he arrived at the lodge at dawn in answer to Glenn's urgent message.

"The term *shadhoobaba* means 'meditating hermit.' Self-styled holy men of all kinds and lots of misfits who just can't get along in the world go off to live alone. Here in Asia such denial is associated with some kind of mystic powers and many hermits are called *shadhoobaba*. It doesn't refer to any one in particular unless you have someone particular in mind. It's like your saying that someone went to church. It could be any church unless you meant one special one."

Glenn was hoarse, his senses nearly as dulled as Liz's. But unlike Liz, he wore a stifling shroud of guilt. He sat at the table, bleary-eyed, ignoring the cup of tea Raanaa had put before him. Raanaa, who had been the first to discover that the children were missing, had already removed four cups that Glenn had allowed to grow cold.

"Which one could Pamela have meant? Where are the closest ones?"

Manik and Masu were conferring with several villagers who stood on the steps of the veranda. Ever since the alarm had been given and Masu, Manik, Ata and Satwyne had hurried to the lodge, there had been a steady stream of visitors, some summoned for special knowledge they had of the surrounding country and others volunteering their help.

Ata went to Manik and addressed him in Bengali. The elder excused himself for a minute and went back to questioning the men on the steps. After a brief conversation he came back into the kitchen.

"There are no hermits near the village that we know about. There may be one to the north, in the ruins up there."

"How far is it?"

Here at least was something Glenn could work on. The sodden blanket of fear that had been smothering him since he awoke to Raanaa's alarm began to lift slightly.

"By river it's thirty miles. It's less by land. Perhaps twenty, maybe a little more."

"What's between here and the ruins? What kind of country is it?"

Manik hesitated for a moment and looked searchingly at Ata. Ata nodded slightly and raised his eyebrows. Manik's answer, although only one word long, said all that had to be said. No other word in any language could more eloquently have conveyed the extremity of the children's peril.

"Jungle."

Glenn knew the answer before Manik said it. He had known it all along. There was little but jungle in any direction once one left the confines of Pukmaranpur, for the village was an island in a suffocating sea of green. The word sounded like a sentence of death. It was no longer the academic description of a type of topography; it described a monster of staggering proportions that had just eaten his child alive.

15

The Walls of the *Mondir*

Satwyne had been gone from the lodge for nearly an hour when the cheers of the gathered villagers signaled his return. Glenn and Liz ran to the front door to see what had happened. Satwyne was on Bolo Bahadur; Oroon, who was to have left Pukmaranpur that day, was on Sabal Kali; Ma was on Begam Bahar and Kala on Sikander. The recent captives were rocking back and forth, coiling and uncoiling their trunks nervously. The sudden outburst had startled them and they were being held in place only by the encouraging chatter of their *mahouts* and occasional light jabs of the *ankus*. Manik spoke to the four mounted men in Bengali and turned back to Glenn.

"They're heading to the four points of the compass. Satwyne invites you to join him. He's going north. He knows the ruins."

Glenn turned to Liz who stood just behind him, her face expressionless, her eyes hollow. She seemed detached, involved in her own nightmares.

"Go ahead, Glenn. I'm too numb to know what's going on. Just bring them back to me."

He took her in his arms and held her close. He was frightened by the ice in her voice and by her rigid body. She seemed to be accusing him; and he had already tried and convicted himself.

Glenn looked up to find Ata's eyes on him. Ata nodded and stepped forward to take Liz from him. As Glenn raced down the veranda steps Satwyne barked a command and Bolo Bahadur raised his right front leg at a steep angle. Glenn stepped onto the elephant's foot and rode up with it. He walked up the rest of the leg, reaching for Satwyne's outstretched hand. As he settled into place the *bor phandi* turned to him darkly and spoke two abrupt sentences in Bengali. Satwyne had made a vow. If anything happened to either child he would kill the men who had driven them from the village. Glenn was too distracted to care. His mind was of the West; he was less fatalistic, more interested in finding his daughter alive than in planning the revenge for her death.

With almost imperceptible commands Satwyne directed Bolo Bahadur across the paddy fields north of the village. Within five minutes they had passed into the forest and the sun had disappeared from overhead.

It was shortly after eleven when Pamela awoke. Khoka was still asleep and she called to him softly. The boy stirred and turned to face her.

"*Hae*, Paamela. *Kota bejeche?*"

"Nearly noon I think." The rays of sun filtering through a small break in the canopy overhead were coming almost straight down.

"We had better find the *mondir* soon. We don't want to get there when it's dark."

"*Accha.* We can go now."

As Khoka moved to stand Sarang rolled over on his back and wiggled his rump from side to side with a satisfied, sighing growl. He flopped on his side and lay there looking up at the children. He still had a great deal of the kitten about him.

It suddenly occurred to Pamela that they hadn't discussed their plans or their destination with their guide.

"Khoka, did you tell Sarang that we wanted him to take us to the *Shadhoobaba?*"

"That is not needed. Sarang knows what we think."

Pamela wasn't at all sure she agreed, but decided against arguing. It was a little late to start worrying about details.

They hadn't gone more than a thousand yards from their resting spot by the tree when Sarang braked to a stop. From a few dozen yards away came the sound of movement so loud and clear that nothing but an elephant, or elephants, could be responsible for it. Before they could decide what to do they heard a human voice call out and another answer from a short distance to their left. A bush about ten yards ahead of them parted and a small, compactly built tusker stepped through with a very dark, slight *mahout* positioned on his neck.

He saw them almost immediately and halted his elephant with an abrupt command. He leaned forward, staring in disbelief, and then called to his partner, who was still hidden behind the screen of vegetation. He spoke so rapidly that Pamela couldn't follow him, although she heard the word *baghh* repeated several times. There was a thrashing movement behind another bush and the second elephant and *mahout* appeared. The elephants were disturbed by the presence of the tiger and the *mahouts* were having trouble holding them still.

"Khoka, it's two men on elephants. Ask them where the *mondir* is. Maybe we could help Sarang find it sooner."

Before Khoka could reply one of the *mahouts* called to them. Again Pamela could recognize the word *baghh* but little else. The other man laughed.

"They say that we shouldn't walk through the forest with a tiger and frighten people's elephants."

"Ask them about the temple, Khoka! Ask them if they know the *Shadhoobaba*."

Khoka hesitated before complying. A stranger come upon suddenly was something very different to him from what it would be to a sighted child. In technologically enriched cultures children learn to relate to voices while still very young. But Khoka had never heard a radio or a telephone and a new voice in his world of gray limbo was perplexing and sometimes even frightening.

The first *mahout* spoke slowly and thoughtfully. Pamela was able to understand much of what he said now that he was measuring his words and speaking less colloquially. He told them there was a *mondir* five or six miles away but that he didn't know whether or not anyone lived there. He told them that if they continued as they were headed they would come to a stream and that they should turn left and walk along the bank until they came to a small waterfall. If they crossed above the falls and continued on away from the stream for another mile he assured them they would come to the ruins.

"*Sukria*," Khoka called, and Pamela echoed his thanks. The men turned their elephants and headed toward the west. When they were about fifty yards off one of them called back to them. Pamela missed the meaning of what had apparently been some kind of warning. Khoka explained: "They said we must be alert and not approach the *mondir* after nightfall. A leopard lives there and is very ferocious."

For nearly an hour they continued northward without interruption but as they came to a place where the ground began to descend into a small valley, Sarang stopped and listened. Again, off in the brush, they could hear the sounds of a large animal moving about. It occurred to Pamela that not all of the elephants they might encounter would necessarily be carrying men on their backs. They were, after all, in wild elephant country, and she recalled with a sense of foreboding that elephants and tigers do not get along very well. It is only under the most unusual circumstances that a tiger, even the largest specimen, will attempt to tackle an adult elephant, but many calves are lost each year to the marauding cats and there is a profound hatred between the two species in the wild.

Pamela's premonition was justified; hardly had the thought occurred to her when a lone tusker, a very large and obviously old animal, emerged from between two trees about fifty yards ahead of them. He was terribly wrinkled and very heavily built. He carried one heavy tusk but his other was a mere stick, the result of an accident long ago. Even at that distance Pamela could see that the huge animal's cheeks were stained a dark color. She did not know that the lone tusker was in *musth,* a condition approaching insanity that is associated with the male elephant's sexual cycle.

Pamela whispered frantically to Khoka, who seemed bewildered. A note of alarm in another's voice can be doubly frightening to a blind person.

"*Hati,* Khoka, wild *hati!* A tusker. Quick, before he sees us!"

Pamela had heard stories from her father and Ata about the danger lone wild elephants sometimes pose, and she was frantic to find cover before they were spotted. The tusker obviously sensed that something was wrong. He shuffled back and forth, flapping his ears and blasting air through his trunk. Time after time he threw his trunk up to test the air. Each time he would spin around, looking for the source of the disturbing signals he was getting. He was grumbling loudly, slowly working himself up into a murderous temper.

Spurred by fear, Pamela thought fast: Khoka, she realized, would be helpless to save himself if the elephant spotted them, and it seemed almost certain now that he would. About twenty feet to their left was a fig tree, wrapped round and round with heavy vines. Figuring it would be the easiest tree to climb and encouraged by the stoutness of the trunk, she grabbed Khoka by the arm and whispered urgently in his ear.

"Run, Khoka, run as fast as you can! We have to climb a tree!"

She wrenched Khoka's hand free from Sarang's harness and pulled him along after her. He stumbled and fell and as she stooped to help him she heard the single shrill blast announcing the tusker's charge. He had spotted them and was charging, trunk and tail straight out. Pamela shoved Khoka against the tree and screamed for him to reach. Obeying automatically, Khoka threw his arms over his head and felt along the trunk until his fingers found the heavy vine that spiraled upward around the tree. Shoving Khoka ahead of her Pamela began climbing as fast as she could. Twice Khoka lost his footing and dangled momentarily until his blindly groping toes could get a purchase on the vine again. Twice Pamela stopped to help him. They reached a thick branch twenty feet off the ground and stood on it with their backs pressed against the massive tree. The mad tusker circled below and had reached up with his trunk just as Khoka had pulled his feet up out of danger. The tusker was enraged now and trumpeted his anger again and again. The volume was shattering. Pamela had never heard anything like it, and what little composure she had left after their frantic climb for safety disintegrated. She wept openly.

"Paamela, Paamela," Khoka crooned. "*Hati* can't climb a tree. He will go away soon but first he must tell us that he is king here."

But the elephant wasn't through with them. Still infuriated, and driven senseless by his condition, he pressed his forehead against the tree and dug in with his hind legs. Eight thousand pounds of brute animal inflamed with the desire to kill, to destroy anything it could get at, surged forward. Pamela could see him straining and for a moment she thought she felt the tree move. But it was her imagination; the tree held. It was old and strong; its roots went deep. Rumbling terribly, the tusker backed off a dozen feet and stood staring at them, exhaling loudly through his trunk. His eyes reflected the hatred he felt for the intruders and his frustration at not being able to snatch them and grind them into the forest floor.

"Paamela? Sarang *kothay*?"

For the first time Pamela realized that she hadn't seen Sarang since she pulled Khoka's hand free of his harness. She had turned her back on the tiger as she ran for the tree and hadn't thought about him since. She began looking for him, almost afraid of what she might find, but her fears were short-lived. There, about twenty feet away, Sarang lay along a branch in another fig tree at least as thick as their own.

"Sarang's in a tree like ours, Khoka." Then she thought for a moment. "Khoka, I didn't know tigers climbed trees."

"Neither do boys without eyes, Paamela, unless *hati* is after them."

The tusker gave no sign of quitting the area. Twice more he tested their tree and once he tested the tree Sarang was in. As he approached the tiger's tree the cat stood on his perch, staring down malevolently at the gray hulk below. For one awful instant Pamela was sure that he was going to leap onto the elephant's back. She called to him frantically:

"No, Sarang, no!"

The tiger didn't jump but he did make some particularly fierce sounds. Pamela was quite startled by their volume and ferocity.

"Is *hati* still there, Paamela?"

It was two hours later and the heat of the day was at its worst.

"*Hae*, Khoka. I can see him hiding. He's waiting for us to come down."

"Is there water near?"

"I don't think so. We aren't near the river yet."

"Good. Then *hati* will soon be thirsty and leave us."

"I'm thirsty, too, Khoka . . . and hungry."

It was the first time either of them had mentioned food. They sat on the broad limb of the fig tree feeling very hungry indeed, and more than a little sorry for themselves.

Pamela didn't know how long she had been dozing

but she came to with a start and nearly cried out when she realized that she was twenty feet above the ground. She was surprised to see that Sarang had come up into their tree and was lying along the branch with his head in Khoka's lap. Khoka was dozing, too.

Pamela looked around carefully. There wasn't a sign of the tusker anywhere. She reached out and touched Khoka's foot.

"Khoka. Khoka, wake up. He's gone."

"I know he has gone. Sarang came and told me."

Pamela climbed down first and Sarang glided silently to the earth beside her. She reached up and guided Khoka's foot back onto the vine from which it had slipped as he followed her down.

Somewhere in the mad scramble that had followed the elephant charge Sarang had lost his harness but they decided against stopping to look for it. If they wanted to find the *Shadhoobaba* before nightfall, and neither of them found the idea of entering the temple after dark very appealing, they would have to push on.

In another three-quarters of an hour they came to the stream the *mahout* had described and they turned to their left. About a quarter of a mile upstream they came to the small waterfall and above it there was an easy ford where they could walk on rocks most of the way.

Although it was late in the afternoon it was still hot

and Pamela looked longingly at the small pools of clear water above the falls. She felt dirty and sticky and longed to dive in and let the cool water sweep over her.

"Khoka. Let's wash in the stream. There are shallow pools and we can take just five minutes."

Khoka agreed readily enough and sat down and began pulling off his shorts.

"Khoka! We have to turn our backs before we undress!"

"Why, Paamela?"

"Because we have to."

Then Khoka understood. He made a soft aaing sound and said:

"You have to turn your back. But I don't."

"Yes, you have to, too."

"Why?"

Pamela thought about it for a minute. She wasn't quite sure why but a sense of propriety isn't always the easiest thing to explain to someone who obviously doesn't have one of his own, or who wants to make such a delicate matter a subject of logical conversation.

"Don't ask silly questions," she said sternly. "You must turn your back as well."

Khoka shrugged, turned until his back was to her, and continued undressing. He felt his way down to the edge of the stream and slipped into a pool. He could hear Pamela splashing nearby. Sarang moved in beside him and lay down in the cool, clean water.

"Paamela. Are you looking at me?"

Pamela's reply was quick and defensive.

"I most certainly am *not!*"

Khoka began giggling softly to himself. He rolled over and lay on top of Sarang, then reached out until he found the cat's face and began washing it until the cat splashed noisily out of the pool to find a more peaceful one of his own. Then Khoka lay back in the pool and laughed aloud.

"What's so funny?"

"I'm not looking at you either. But I know why. I know all about that."

On the far side of the ford they came upon a narrow path that cut through the thick stream-side tangle. About a hundred yards along the trail Pamela came to a stop. They had again entered a cathedral-like area where the tall trunks of the trees soared upward without obstruction to a green-black canopy overhead. There was practically no undergrowth at all here and it was possible to see for hundreds of feet in all directions. No rays of light filtered through and the whole area was bathed in a uniform greenness that gave the impression of being underwater. Indeed, it was rather like being at the bottom of a vast sea.

Somewhere overhead a bird chuckled, shrieked, then chuckled again. Off to their right a smaller bird trilled three times, then called *whisp, whisp, wheep* in a confidential tone. Near where they stood a small underground brook bubbled at the surface for about a dozen yards and the ground around was spongy with black mud and a light sprinkling of leaves. In the mud Pamela could see the clear imprint of an elephant's foot. Even she could tell that it was a fresh track, for it hadn't yet filled with water, although the depressed ground was oozing. On the far side of the open wood she could just make out two slender monoliths that apparently had once guarded a kind of gateway.

"Khoka. *Hati* sign. There's a fresh footprint and the forest is open here. There aren't any trees we can climb. What will we do if it's another tusker?"

"Are we near the *mondir*?"

"I think so. I can see a gate or something up ahead."

"Then the animals here are friends of the *Shadhoobaba*. They will not harm us unless he tells them to and then trees would not matter. We have come this far, Paamela, we must go all the way to the *mondir*."

Pamela looked carefully at Sarang but he didn't give any sign of being alarmed and she started through the cathedral wood. The spongy floor absorbed any sounds they made, and except for a periodic and slightly demented chuckling overhead all was silent.

Pamela stopped to examine the two monoliths that

towered over them when they came to the ancient gateway. They were much taller than they appeared to be from a distance and were covered with small animal-like figures. The relief was not deep but the carving was intricate and the figures overlapped each other in a kind of orgiastic movement. Small vines and tendrils interlaced the shallow figures, and lizards by the dozens scampered up and down the narrow avenues that had been chiseled into the stone longer ago than anyone knew.

There was a rustling nearby and Pamela stiffened as she saw Sarang's head turn sharply sidewise. A large porcupine ambled out of a brush pile and crossed the path in front of them.

"*Shaujaroo*, Khoka."

"He is a messenger. The *Shadhoobaba* knows we are here."

The forest beyond the monoliths seemed different to Pamela. It was lighter and the trees were not as tall. Here and there the canopy was open to the sky and sunlight fell to earth in broad splashes of light. Although she could not tell from where they stood, they had entered a vast courtyard. Walls ran off from the gateposts she had stopped to examine, but they had crumbled with time and were covered with brush. The children started along what appeared to be a path. Off to the right a snorting and crashing behind the brush announced the departure of a wild sow and her young. Khoda whispered hoarsely to Pamela that it was another messenger, and they kept moving forward.

Pamela began noticing large pieces of stone half buried in the vines and brush beside the pathway. Occasionally she thought she recognized animalistic forms in the exposed portions but she didn't stop to examine them. She was staring ahead, expecting at any moment either to see the *mondir* or to be struck down by the wrath of the *Shadhoobaba*. She began to wonder seriously whether or not he would find them worthy.

The trail was narrow. Pamela led the way. Sarang came next with Khoka behind him, clinging resolutely to the black and orange tail with both hands. Pamela called back over her shoulder in a whisper, describing the area through which they were moving.

They came to a second pair of monoliths, almost exact duplicates of the first. It was the entrance to an inner courtyard and here the walls that ran off to the east and west were still apparent. At set intervals along the wall Pamela could see small carved figures. She could not recognize the demon faces as representing anything she had ever seen. They seemed to be part man, part animal.

"There are long walls, Khoka, and lots of carved stones."

They passed through the second gateway and then Pamela saw it. Before her lay an avenue bordered with dozens of carved human and animal figures. A few of them had tumbled to the ground and seemed to be wrestling with vines that entwined them in a green and brown stranglehold, but most of them were still standing, even though they were leaning precariously inward toward the avenue. At the end of the path, what appeared to be a mountain of vine-laced rock soared upward into the trees. It was terraced on the three sides visible to Pamela, and brush and smaller trees grew on every level. Pamela stared ahead into the gloom and her eyes became wide as the details of the ancient temple began to emerge. It was a mass of carving; every facet of every rock in the giant, ragged pyramid was covered with deeply incised figures. She edged forward slowly and more details began to emerge. The entire structure looked like a mass of animal and humanlike creatures locked in an agony of writhing combat. The jungle's encroachment added the unneeded touch of a million vine tendrils snaking their way through the confusion, strangling a man here, a leopard there. The vines, the rocks, the whole massive creation hissed at them as thousands of lizards scurried across its endless faces. Although Pamela could not see them, scores of snakes also made their home in the vicinity of the great pyramid, thriving on the lizards and the rats that nested in the natural caves formed by man-hewn rock and in the growing things that marked the jungle's reclamation. Although the men, perhaps even the race of men, who had built the giant edifice were dead, the structure itself was alive, a cogent element in the complicated ecology of the jungle.

"Khoka, the temple! We have found the temple!"

"If the *Shadhoobaba* has not stopped us now he must have found us worthy. We must find the way in."

Pamela began inching forward. Of all the uncertain moments she had lived through since leaving the lodge in the middle of the night, this was the worst. She looked up at the great temple that loomed larger and more forbidding with each step they took. She was too absorbed to look to either side but even if she had, she probably would not have seen the two men that stood off behind a screen of brush, watching them. Four eyes followed their progress with deep and abiding interest. Only extraordinary willpower held the men back from rushing toward the children who had been the object of their frantic day-long search.

16

The *Shadhoobaba*

Inside, the *Shadhoobaba* waited. He indeed knew of their coming, although the messengers who had brought him the news were of a different sort than Pamela or Khoka might have imagined. In the rank little room he had preempted long ago for his living quarters the old man sat and waited. The old temple, quiet except for the dry, scaly rustling of the snakes and lizards with which he shared the ruins, would echo to human footsteps even though the visitors were barefoot. Seeping water from a thousand monsoons was working its way down through the layers of applied rock; and the penetrating roots of the trees and brush, to which this once massive testimony to the genius of man was now nothing but a rocky hill, were having their way. The inside of the temple was beginning to crumble, for the rocks themselves were rotting, peeling, giving way to hostile forces. Already rooms further into the great pyramid were unsafe, for root-loosened blocks of carved stone were slipping inward, preparing to collapse. The floor of the corridor along which the children would come was littered with fallen rock and their approach could not be silent.

Overhead, in the great vaults that soared up and out of sight, there were faint whispers of movement and soft confidential squeals. The bats which used the tallest portions of the stepped tower were seldom still; now, since it was almost dusk, they emerged from every crack and crevice to fill the sky with a cloud of buoyant gray. In places within the temple their droppings were several feet deep. The stench was remarkable.

The man was a hermit, and, indeed, he did a great deal of meditating. But most of his thoughts lingered on the tragedy that had driven him away from the world of the living. He still sought a meaning for the deaths of his parents, his sister, his wife and their three young children, which had occurred when smallpox ravaged his village three decades earlier. He had come here then to search for a meaning and, never having found it, he stayed on. In time the thought of rejoining a world of strangers became abhorrent to him and he had become a permanent inhabitant of a dead world. Since everyone he had ever cared about was dead, there was a sad logic to his residence in the halls of death. He belonged here with his bitter memories, accountable to no one but his conscience, competing with no one, asking help of his gods alone, and that only in the form of a final sleep they had so far refused to award him.

He did not object to the two or three people a year who stumbled upon his retreat unless they asked questions that probed behind his mask. He did not know, of course, that these same accidental visitors carried away tales of the *Shadhoobaba* and that when these rumors, the soft, windblown flotsam of human imagination, came to rest in ready minds, he was endowed with supernatural powers. Nothing could have been further from the truth. He was a frail old man quite near death, a fact which he sensed with complete satisfaction. He suffered from malnutrition and a severe skin ailment. His sight was failing, he had no teeth, and he smelled as if he hadn't bathed in thirty years, which happened to be the case. It had been over ten years since he had had a single hair on his head. Even his eyebrows and eyelashes were gone. For these and other reasons the *Shadhoobaba* was a remarkable-looking man, quite remarkable enough to play the role he was now called upon to enact. He had listened to the problems of the two visitors who had arrived an hour before the children and agreed to help.

Both Pamela and Khoka gagged when they entered the long passage, and Sarang exhaled violently. The smell was overwhelming. It took them some minutes before they could move forward because Pamela had difficulty adjusting her eyes to the darkness. But, bit by bit, the walls on either side began to take on a discernible texture, and the outline of the passage ahead began to clear. The rubble of the floor hurt their feet, and stones they inadvertently kicked banged against others, creating much more noise than they wanted to make. Their progress was slow, hesitant, reluctant. But there is a time, even in the lives of children, when it is impossible to turn back, when the commitment alone matters.

"Tumi ki cao?"

The *Shadhoobaba's* voice echoed down the passageway like a roll of thunder. Both children gasped aloud and Khoka stumbled ahead to grab Pamela's arm. Even Sarang was brought up short and issued an abrupt comment that was half snort and half growling cough.

Impatiently the voice again demanded to know their mission.

"Tumi ki cao?"

Khoka nudged Pamela, who answered in English without thinking. She called, hesitantly, but quite loudly for one so badly frightened, "We have come to see the *Shadhoobaba*."

"*Apni kake can?*"

"*Shadhoobaba*."

"*Tomar nam ki?*"

"*Amar nam Pamela*."

"*Chele?*"

"*Amar nam Khoka*."

"*Baghh?*"

"*Sarang*."

"*Tomra aso*."

On his order to advance the children moved forward slowly. Pamela could make out the flickering light of a small fire ahead. She had terrible misgivings about what she might see when she entered the chamber at the end of the corridor. The brief exchange they had just engaged in had somehow been safer with her words echoing down the corridor and his tumbling back. It wasn't the same as an actual confrontation with so terrifying a figure, so awesome a concept. The fact that the *mondir* did exist, and had a voice, was confirmation of the entire *Shadhoobaba* legend. It was now unthinkable for either child to question any part of it.

When they got to the archway that obviously opened into the *Shadhoobaba's* inner sanctum, Pamela stopped. She reached back and took Khoka by the arm and he came abreast of her. She took a deep breath and heard Khoka imitate her gesture of preparation as they stepped forward together. If the smell in the corridor was remarkable, here in the inner chamber it was stupefying. For a moment the light of the flickering fire blinded Pamela, but slowly her eyes adjusted and she could see the skeletal figure of the *Shadhoobaba* sitting on a raised stone platform about fifteen feet from where they stood. He was cross-legged on a pile of filthy rags, naked except for a length of cloth that rested in his lap. The old man raised a bony hand and beckoned to them. Their movement created small currents of air that played upon the low flames of the fire by his side. The dancing reflections on the carved rock walls made the room seem alive with a host of phantoms. Pamela steeled herself to the task that lay before her.

"Tomra aso."

The old man beckoned to them to come closer. When they were no more than five feet away he held up his hand, palm out, and they stopped. Pamela pulled Khoka back a step to keep him in line with her. Sarang came forward and sat down next to Khoka, leaning slightly against his leg and watching the old man warily.

"Why do you seek the *Shadhoobaba?*"

At first Pamela couldn't make out why she was puzzled. It didn't dawn on her for the moment, but then she realized.

"You . . . you speak English!"

"What is there about your tongue that should keep the *Shadhoobaba* from knowing it?"

"Nothing. Nothing, *sir*."

"You may speak any tongue you wish here."

"Oh, no thank you. English will be fine."

"Why do you seek me?"

The old man stared down at Pamela with rheumy eyes that had already seen too much for one lifetime. How very like her she is, he thought. He was thinking of the daughter of the British officer who had commanded his regiment in northern India nearly half a century earlier. He had been a sergeant then, but that was a lifetime away. A great sadness filled him as he recalled the brave officer's collapse when the child had died in a cholera epidemic that had swept the fort. How very, very like her she is, he thought. Like seeing a ghost.

"We have questions that we cannot answer."

"How many questions?"

"Just two."

"And you, *chele*, they are your questions as well?"

"*Hae*. They are my questions."

"What is the first?"

Khoka hesitated. He fully believed that any answer he found in this room would be the answer he would have to live with for the rest of his life. For him this was the court of last appeal. He gathered his courage and spoke softly. The sweat was standing out on his face and he could feel it trickling down his back. He gripped Sarang by the scruff for support.

"Will my eyes ever return?"

There was a long pause. Although Khoka didn't know it, the old man was staring at him. Then he answered slowly, softly, in a more gentle voice than he had used in his first challenge to them.

"Is your Lord the living Buddha?"

Khoka nodded affirmatively.

"Recall the Buddha's words before his death: 'Be ye lamps unto yourselves. Rely on yourselves, and do not rely on external help. Hold fast to the truth as a lamp.' "

Khoka recalled the words but didn't understand the context. The old man continued: "Here is your truth, here is your lamp. Rely on it . . . You *may* see again. It will be given to you to perform a miracle. Believe in it, wait on it. When the time comes, if you succeed, your eyes will awaken. They are only resting."

Khoka was desperate to ask about the miracle, to ask how he would know when the time had come, but the old man cut him off before he could find the words.

"What is your second question?"

Khoka was still lingering over the old man's first answer when Pamela spoke up.

"The people of Pukmaranpur are angry with our tiger. They say he'll turn on them. We know that he

won't, but the villagers are afraid and want him put in
a cage or sent away. What can we do?"

The old man started to answer but before his first
word was out Sarang gave a mighty yawn and sank
to his belly. Sarang was famous back at the hunting
lodge for the noise of his yawns, a kind of half-
hearted, muffled roar, and coming suddenly as it did
in the closed chamber, it was quite startling. The old
man nearly smiled but caught himself in time. It
would have been the first time he had smiled in a very
long time. He tipped his head slightly and looked at
Pamela again. How very, very like her she is, he
thought. How strange that it should be here, after so
long a time. He himself had lifted the body of the dead
child out of her father's arms and placed her gently
in the grave with all the others. And now, it seemed,
she was before him again.

"Your tiger will harm no one."

Pamela felt a great wave of hope flood over her.
She was delighted for Khoka, and now *this* news.

The *Shadhoobaba* continued gently, his voice
breaking slightly as he spoke, "But the tiger's place
is not among people. There is no way to remove the
fear he causes even in the hearts of the bravest men.
Take him to the forest and show him his rightful place,
for there he is a king. Perhaps he will let you come to
him from time to time. He will be grateful to you for
returning him to his kingdom."

Pamela was not as bitterly disappointed as she

thought she would be. Somehow it seemed right, coming as it did from this ancient. Still, there was a question in her mind.

"He has been free to go all along. Why hasn't he gone before now, if that's what he wants?"

The old man didn't want to engage in a dialogue. That was not the part he was playing. Still, he could answer this one question and, if anything, strengthen his pronouncement.

"His body has been free to go but you have held his heart a prisoner. You must free *all* of him. A king without a heart is not a king at all."

There was a finality to the pronouncement and Pamela, for once in her life, could not think of a rebuttal.

The old man raised his hand again. Sarang sprang up at the gesture and watched him guardedly.

"I must summon someone to take you home. It will be night when you leave this temple and a leopard waits in the forest beyond the second gate. He is not our friend."

The hermit closed his eyes tightly for a moment then dropped his hand. His voice was shaky as he spoke.

"Go . . . now. Go!"

He didn't answer as the children called their thanks to him. He watched as they backed out of the chamber, Pamela guiding Khoka into the passageway. Sarang moved on ahead of them. When the old man was sure that he could not be seen he lowered his head. He felt a tear fall onto his hands that were clenched in his lap. It felt hot, as if it would burn into his flesh. He was happy. It had been so long since he had wept that he thought he had forgotten how.

It was night when Pamela, Khoka and Sarang emerged from the passageway. The blessedly clean air swept over them like a lovely, cleansing rain and they instinctively breathed deeply. The cloying odor of the chamber and the passageway slowly left them as the last particles of decay were expelled from their lungs.

Pamela heard a noise and looked up. Something huge was looming up in the brush. Out of the dark an enormous animal was moving toward them. She was rescued from a wave of panic by a familiar and reassuring voice:

"Pamela. I have come to take you home."

The two men slipped down off Bolo Bahadur and she ran toward them, almost pulling Khoka off his feet as she dragged him along. She thrust him at Satwyne and threw herself into her father's arms.

Glenn lifted his face to the sky and thought to himself, God forgive me — and God help me — if she ever finds out!

Back in the grotto the *Shadhoobaba* reached into a small basket. He lifted the treasure out carefully. He stared down at the ragged photograph of three dark children and the tears filled his eyes. It was the one thing he had brought with him from the outside world except his sadness. Somewhere deep within the temple there was a muffled roar as another ceiling caved inward. It was a sound he had heard more frequently of late.

17

Sarang the King

It was just before dawn when Bolo Bahadur broke through the brush and cut across the northern paddy fields with the tiger following behind him. There were fires around the perimeter of the village, fires that had been kept burning to guide the searchers and perhaps even the lost children home. Khoka sat in front of his father, his head lolling forward as he slept. The *bor phandi's* strong arm encircled the boy's waist, holding him in place. Glenn sat behind Satwyne, with Pamela cradled in his arms. It had been hours since he had been able to feel either arm, but he swore to himself that they would drop off before he would shift them and disturb her sleep.

News of the rescue echoed across the fields, started by the fire tenders and relayed from hut to hut. Most of the people had spent the night awake, waiting. Liz and Ata heard the cry where they sat silently waiting on the veranda. As if propelled, Liz sped down the steps and along the path to the dikes, tears streaming down her cheeks. At the end of the last dike she leaped into the paddy and ran through the knee-deep water until she threw herself against the side of Bolo Bahadur. On command the *koonki* knelt, first with his hind legs and then with his fore. Glenn slipped off and gently transferred Pamela into Liz's arms. The first rays of the sun were slipping over the treetops to the east and the tears glistened on Liz's cheeks.

The *koonki* stood and moved off slowly toward the village. Satwyne was taking his son home. For a moment the tiger hesitated, then followed the elephant. The people gathered along the dikes watched the strange procession pass without comment. Satwyne stared over their heads, refusing to acknowledge their presence.

It was three o'clock in the afternoon when Pamela awoke. A hot bath, clean clothes and her favorite meal of Raanaa's special fish soup were waiting. Liz and Glenn had decided not to punish her, not even to bring up the subject of her desperately foolish act until she was ready to discuss it. They didn't have long to wait. She came to them of her own accord before supper and delivered herself haltingly but sincerely of a speech she had obviously rehearsed in the privacy of her bedroom. She realized, she said, how wrong and foolish she had been and she promised never to do anything like it again. She also said that she and Khoka were ready to let Sarang go back to the forest, where he belonged.

Neither Satwyne nor the Barclays put any restriction on their children's meeting again. It was, though, two days before they saw each other. Neither of them wanted to be very far from home. To satisfy herself that all was well, Liz had gone down to the *bor phandi's* hut to see Khoka while Pamela was asleep. Khoka was already awake, sitting in front of the hut with his father. They sat facing each other, cross-legged on a woven mat, and ate from bowls of rice and fish. Satwyne motioned to her when he saw her approaching and she knelt quietly beside the little boy and kissed him on the forehead. He reached up and felt her face and whispered softly:

"*Adab, Mama.*"

"*Adab, Khoka,*" she answered. In a little while she walked slowly back to the lodge.

Through Manik and Masu, Glenn let the word be spread throughout the village that the tiger was going to be returned to the forest. The news was greeted with a general feeling of relief. Even those who had not been actively involved in the opposition felt that the matter had gone quite far enough. There had already been dissension, threats of violence, and a near tragedy that could be laid to the matter. There are other ways in which a tiger can cause harm to people, it was agreed, besides direct attack.

At noon on the third day Khoka walked slowly up the path leading to the lodge. His hand rested on Sarang's shoulders and the half-grown cat moved in the stately pace he had learned to use when walking with the boy alone. Many villagers turned to watch them pass but no comments were made.

Liz greeted him at the top of the steps and Khoka and Sarang went on into the lodge as they had done so many times before. Quietly, without any outward sign of her feelings, Pamela came forward and knelt before the tiger. She patted him, rubbed her nose against his, and as she stood she moistened her fingers and rubbed briskly on a small stain that marred the white spot behind his right ear. Glenn came into the room and Liz nodded to him. Neither of them said anything; they waited for the children to take the lead.

Solemnly, even reassuringly, Pamela turned to her parents. She was determined to see the mission through without losing her dignity.

"We'll be back in a little while. We're going to the last paddy field, beyond the hill. It's near the glen, Daddy, where you had your *pilkhana*. We won't have to go into the forest."

Liz and Glenn stood on the veranda, watching as the two children and the tiger walked down the path away from the lodge. They turned left where the east-west dike intersected the high bank and walked single file out between the fields. Liz's hand was in Glenn's and she pressed her head hard against his arm.

On the hill, the highest hill in the area except for the one on which the Buddhist shrine stood, Satwyne sat cross-legged on the back of his giant *koonki*. In his right hand he held open a black umbrella that shielded his head from the sun. In his left he held a small bundle of leaves his blind son had rolled and tied and given to him. It contained a few orange hairs that the boy had plucked from the coat of his pet, the king. From his vantage point, Satwyne had a clear view of the children as they walked around the hill on the hard-packed embankment that had known the passage of men for hundreds of years, but on very different missions. He watched until they were three small dots on the farthest dike at the edge of the farthest field. Then, alone except for Bolo Bahadur, Satwyne spoke softly to Riboy. He told his dead wife how sorry he was that he had allowed pain to come into their son's life and he promised her, as he had so often done before, that he would devote his life to Khoka's welfare.

The children and their tiger passed the cleared area where the newly captured elephants had once been tethered, near the shelter that had been erected when the beautiful Begam Bahar had almost died from the strange sickness. Overhead the kestrel circled in her endless patrol for mice to feed the nestlings secreted away in the tallest tree at the forest's edge. Pamela did not turn to watch and missed her plunging dive into the field behind them. She barely heard the distant *ki-ki-ki-wee* of the tiercel's congratulations.

When they reached the far edge of the field the children sat in the shade of a single large tree that had been left standing when the area had been taken from the jungle many years before. The area had been fallow for several seasons and was overgrown with weeds. Long before the jungle could reclaim the land, however, it would be cleared and tilled, almost surely with the help of the elephants that were now working a regular day in the fields.

Pamela waited for Khoka to speak first. Sarang was really his pet and it was up to him, she felt, to handle the affair as he saw fit.

Khoka sat with his face to the sun, his hand resting on the shoulder of his tiger. Sarang lay by his side. Softly, in Bengali, Khoka addressed him:

"Here is the forest, Sarang, and here you are king. You must go back to where you belong. Your heart is free and you are a tiger again. We will listen for your call and we will come to watch for you here in the field but you may never come into the village again. You are not a king there but a stranger and you are not welcome. You are prepared to love men but men are not ready to love you, for they cannot love what they do not understand. It is easier for us to fear than to love and that is why you are a king and I am not. It is time for you to go."

It would be many years before Pamela would be able to comprehend just how remarkable Khoka's speech had been. At the time she was fighting so desperately to hold back her tears that it didn't really register. Years later she would try to remember it, just as it had been spoken, and would write down her reconstruction to the best of her ability to be sure that she would never forget it again.

As Khoka stood, Sarang rolled over and came to his feet.

"Wait, Khoka, wait."

Pamela knelt in front of the tiger and reached into the pocket of her shorts. She removed a necklace she had prepared and tied it securely around Sarang's neck. It was stoutly made of heavy twine, carefully braided and twisted.

"Here, Khoka," she said, and placed the boy's hand on the symbol she had created of Sarang's authority. Khoka slipped his hands around the woven bands until his fingers came to a series of hard, familiar objects.

"Your bracelet, Paamela! You have given Sarang your bracelet!"

How often he and Pamela had sat together with

that bracelet, his inquiring fingers memorizing each charm as Pamela had explained again and again: her father's baby ring, her grandfather's cuff link with the tiny diamond chip, the small, rough amethyst Liz had brought back from Canada, Glenn's fraternity pin and the small ladybug pin that had belonged to Liz's grandmother. Each piece was a treasure, almost as much so to Khoka as to Pamela, and he knew better than anyone else what a gift of love it was.

Sarang made no effort to follow them back to the village. The single word of command that Khoka gave him when he ordered him to go was not within the working vocabulary the tiger normally understood, yet he remained where they left him. They would never know how long he stayed there, for Pamela did not turn around.

As they neared the lodge she said, "Now, Khoka, we must see about your Miracle. It's time your eyes woke up."

"Paamela. Where do you look for a Miracle?"

"I don't know. But we'll find one somewhere."

And there was absolutely no doubt in either of their minds that they would.

18

Search for a Miracle

The trouble with Sarang, culminating in the children's nearly disastrous escapade, cut into Glenn's schedule, but through it all ran the elephant project. For Glenn it was a time of learning. Capturing the elephants had been only a small part of the problem. His primary task was to develop practical techniques for applying the power he now had at his disposal. Presumably, elephants could always be made available in other agricultural communities, but means had to be devised for converting their strength so that they could earn their keep. In a subsistence economy an elephant could easily become the most intolerable of luxuries unless it could increase the output of the community enough to pay for itself. The margin above that point would be the profit and the measure of that profit alone would prove or disprove the validity of the whole experiment.

Sikander had the pulling power of about fifty healthy men, and this was without really straining. Although Begam Bahar was both younger and smaller, she was able to do nearly as much work. Her superior build made her immensely powerful for her size. There were no practical tasks that required more strength than this, so the exercise was strictly one of conversion. The first problem had come when the elephants were put to pulling plows. Their great feet crushed the ridges between the furrows and offset much of the good that they did. It became a problem of teaching them where to walk. Fortunately they responded easily to their *mahouts'* gentle prodding. An elephant is naturally careful about where he puts his feet because of his great weight, and the two trainees responded successfully to this aspect of their schooling.

Shortly after his arrival at Pukmaranpur, Glenn had surveyed the machinery that had been left behind by the agricultural team and found that most of it was too far gone to be of use. The one piece he felt was critical to his enterprise was the water pump. It would enable many more fields to be used than were then under cultivation. The Gamalbuk River carried more than enough water past Pukmaranpur's front door, but it was thirty feet below the level of the fields. To raise water to that height and then send it along canals covering an area of nearly a square mile would require an enormous amount of energy, and although elephant power could be adapted to this task it would be, Glenn felt, extremely wasteful. There was the problem, too, that elephants do not like doing one simple task over and over again without letup. They get bored, and a bored elephant, Manik explained, can become hard to handle, even dangerous at times. Although Glenn was extremely fond of his two mountaineers he was still somewhat intimidated by them, and the mere mention of possible danger could sway his decision in any matter. It wasn't fear for his own safety, it was his feeling of responsibility for the men who now worked for him. He was categorically opposed to anything that would increase the risks he felt they took every time they took their mounts into the field. It takes a long time, Ata assured him, to accept completely the idea that so large an animal can ever be under the control of anything as puny as a man.

Glenn found that the water pump could be salvaged but the diesel engine that had been brought in to power it was beyond repair. Further investigation, however, revealed that one of the four tractors still had a workable engine, although it would require a major overhaul to put it back into service. It was an easy task for Begam Bahar and Sikander, working together, to haul the disabled giant out of its bed of vines and brush and drag it to the river. A simple pulley was rigged on a thick branch and with hardly any strain at all Sikander, under Kala's direction, walked away from the tree, lifting the engine neatly out of the tractor body. In time this engine was put to work running the water pump and the irrigation ditches ran full.

The elephants proved useful in the building of dikes where the problem was essentially that of moving large amounts of earth. This could be solved by putting the elephants to work using drags much larger than those already used by the men. It became, for the first time, a simple matter to divide a large field or to open up two smaller ones so that they joined. Pieces of tractor body mounted to wooden planks were fashioned into pushing blades of sorts and Sikander and Begam Bahar became animated bulldozers. There seemed to be almost no limit to the adaptability of the elephants as long as their basic strengths were employed. Pulling, pushing, and carrying were the animals' natural talents, and Glenn found the useful variations on these themes almost endless.

Several times after their capture Sikander and Begam Bahar heard wild elephants in the forest not far beyond the village limits. Once or twice their *mahouts* heard trumpeting but for the most part the signals were beyond the auditory range of human beings. The first time it happened both elephants stopped their work and refused to be prodded on. Sikander issued a deep sound like a growl and flapped his ears to show his agitation. Begam Bahar exhaled violently half a dozen times and set up a soft humming noise. It was decided not to press the issue until it became a showdown between man and beast, and the captives were taken to the river and bathed. It was not a good idea to interrupt their normal schedule, but it seemed the lesser of two evils. In time, though, the captives showed less reaction to the calls from beyond the forest's edge and eventually the wild herd moved away.

Shortly after the children's rescue, Satwyne had to leave Pukmaranpur to accept another *mela shikar* contract fifty miles upriver. He had been unwilling to permit Bolo Bahadur to engage in the agricultural enterprise and Glenn readily understood this. Bolo Bahadur was one of the few really experienced *koonkis* in the region and as such was far too valuable to dissipate on less critical jobs. The relationship between Satwyne and his enormously powerful mount was a wondrous thing and, as he explained to Glenn, he didn't want the *koonki* to resent him, which he would surely do if put to anything as demeaning as pulling a plow or tamping a dike day after day.

Oroon had started downriver with Sabal Kali immediately after the children's rescue, so Satwyne's departure left the elephant population of Pukmaranpur at two. But the two had learned well and no longer needed a guard elephant, which is what Bolo Bahadur had been. The night before Satwyne left there was a dinner party at the lodge and Khoka moved in with the Barclays instead of with a rather irritable second cousin, as he had in the past when Satwyne was away from the village.

Not long after Satwyne's departure word arrived at Pukmaranpur that another elephant was available for a very low rental figure. There was a lumber operation about thirty miles northeast of the village and one of the cows in the herd there was found to be pregnant. The gestation period of an elephant is nearly two years and once it is discovered that a cow is pregnant she is taken off all heavy work. The owners of the thirty-year-old Meernah Prue were faced with more than a year of maintenance on an elephant for which there was very little to do in the way of light work around the lumber camp. They had heard of Glenn's experiment and reasoned that their expectant mother could manage the agricultural labors with ease and earn her keep at the same time. The negotiations were surprisingly brief and the *mahout,* Chooni, became a temporary resident of Pukmaranpur as Meernah Prue joined Glenn's experimental herd.

If Glenn thought Sikander and Begam Bahar were

adaptable he was astounded by the new cow's ability. She had been a working elephant for twenty-one years and there seemed to be no job to which she could not apply herself with about half the instruction needed by the two trainees. The work output of the herd was doubled by the addition of this one experienced cow, pregnancy and all, and Glenn began fully to appreciate the potential of elephant power in the growing fields of man.

Westerners, knowing little of elephants and their use, tend to over-romanticize the role of the *mahout*. The mental picture of the slender, dark man perched on his mighty slave's neck might lead one to believe that he is the pick of his society, a member of the village elite. Such is not generally the case, however. A *mahout* in Asia has about the same status that a truck driver enjoys in the West, as a skilled worker who can be hired for a reasonable price to do a solid day's work. Few *mahouts* ever get to own their own elephants and although they are respected for the job they do, they are neither wealthy nor necessarily wise. Somewhat overdone, too, is the Western concept of the relationship between the *mahout* and his elephant. In fact, most *mahouts* feel pretty much about their charges the way truck drivers feel about their trucks.

Glenn felt it essential to his experiment that Ma, Kala, and Chooni take pride in what they did. He couldn't justify this with elephant experience but it was the way he had always worked. Accordingly, he brought them into conferences with Ata, Manik and Masu and gave them a feeling of importance they probably would never have had under a normal program. Not at all surprisingly, the results began to show. The men proved to be interested and cooperative and in very short order began to make suggestions that had real value. Ma and Chooni were experienced *mahouts* but Kala, newly elevated to the rank of elephant driver, worked hard to be both seen and heard. There were times, Glenn thought, when he tried too hard. It would be better, he confided to Ata, if Kala would relax a bit. The experiment with the elephants was also an experiment with men. By and large it seemed to be working on both fronts.

About two weeks after Satwyne's departure the motor launch brought news from the District Commissioner: within the month he would arrive at Pukmaranpur to review the experiment for himself. While this personal attention was flattering to Glenn, and while he looked forward to showing off the progress they had made, the interval became a time of extra effort. What the District Commissioner saw when he arrived would determine what he would say when he got back to Chittagong, and what he would say there would reach the United Nations in New York, the American Embassy in Rawalpindi and the State Department in Washington. Glenn didn't have a job to protect — his company was waiting for him in Wichita when his contract with the United Nations expired — but he did have an image to sustain, his own image of himself. It was that image that had prompted him to accept the strange assignment in the first place. For Glenn, to be without an almost impossible task to accomplish was to be without gainful employment. His ancestors, arriving in Kansas by prairie schooner, had had to fight off Indians with one hand while building cabins with the other. Glenn's grandfather, who had lived with Glenn and his parents for the first thirteen years of Glenn's life, had been a small boy then and had told his grandson many stories of the old days. Here, in Pukmaranpur, as everywhere that Glenn went, he was trying to live up to the image of himself and of his inheritance that those stories had engendered. It is with increasing frustration that men such as he face a world where such an image becomes increasingly difficult to maintain. For Glenn, then, the elephants of Pukmaranpur and the ground they tilled were threads to which he must cling tenaciously. Quite simply, it was a question of pride.

For Liz the coming visit of the Commissioner meant something else, something just as profoundly personal. Her conversations with him would mark the first step in her determined plan to make Khoka her own. The fact that Pamela could be her only natural child rankled no less now than it had nearly eleven years earlier, when her doctor first broke it to her. There had been passing conversations over the years about adopting a child but nothing had come of it because there was no fixed object on which to focus. Khoka, though, *was* a fixed object and Liz found her heart committed to him more and more each day. She found herself no longer concentrating, as she had for over a decade, on her only child. In everything, in planning meals, in organizing activities, and in her letters to her sister, she thought, spoke and wrote of her *children*. The plural form had become natural to her and she was determined that it would never change.

Pamela and Khoka had no idea of where to turn first in their search for a Miracle. They were quite content to follow the *Shadhoobaba's* advice on all counts save one. He had admonished Khoka, when he spoke of the Miracle, to "believe in it, wait on it." The children were prepared to believe in it but not at all ready to wait on it. They would actively seek it out in everything they did, everywhere they went.

They still believed that they were the only people alive who knew what the *Shadhoobaba* had said, and so they determined between them not to discuss the Miracle with anyone. "Besides," Pamela had said, "think what a wonderful surprise it will be for everyone when you show up one day with your eyes working."

To them it was that simple. A Miracle was to be had almost for the asking and eyes that had been useless for seven years would be fully functional again. It never occurred to either of them to question Khoka's ability to perform a Miracle once they found one that needed performing. In a way it was a good thing that they did decide to keep the matter to themselves, for neither Glenn nor Liz, who now shared Glenn's and Satwyne's secret, would have found it easy to live with the children's blissful optimism. The deception, from an adult's point of view, was assuming the proportions of cruelty. To have gone along with it would have been rather like telling a child that his parents would live forever. Adults must face as one of their most difficult tasks the pricking of balloons that the hope-filled souls of children are forever sending aloft. By getting to the *Shadhoobaba* first Glenn and Satwyne had inflated just such a balloon.

Sarang was finding few if any miracles at his disposal in the forests beyond the village. Within thirty hours after the children had abandoned him to his own devices he was desperately hungry and at a loss to know how to feed himself. He made a complete blunder of an attempt to take a boar on his first hunt. He had stalked it well enough, but when he finally got into a position to attack, he made the mistake of standing erect and growling viciously. Before he realized what had happened there was a loud crashing in the dense thicket, and where his first potentially self-obtained meal had stood there were some sharp little hoofprints in the soft, moist soil and nothing more. Under natural conditions he would have remained under his mother's tutelage for upwards of two and a half years — for it takes that long for a tiger to become a tiger — and she would have taught him how to hunt the wild pig.

His next target was a sambar stag, but he never even got to begin his stalk. Almost certainly he would have been unable to make the kill even if he had gotten close. That too is a fine art. The only animal that didn't vanish like the wind at his approach was a very large and very well armed porcupine. He soon learned why. He was now limping badly on his right front paw, the paw he had led with in his abortive assault; and he was still painfully aware of his empty stomach.

He found a small marsh deep in the forest and was able to catch a dozen frogs along its edges. Later that same day, his fourth day on his own, he found two nests full of fledgling red jungle fowl and added these to his diet. It was poor fare for a growing tiger and his condition began to deteriorate.

There are certain signals in an animal's life-drive, particularly an animal as advanced on the evolutionary scale as a tiger, which, although automatic, are almost consciously understood. Somehow, deep down inside, in a way impossible for human beings to comprehend, Sarang *knew* that he had to learn how to hunt. It wasn't *knowledge*, exactly, so much as it was a total response to his predicament. He could not maintain his condition without food, lots of it in steady supply, and he set about the staggering task of teaching himself how to hunt, by night and by day. It became virtually a twenty-four-hour occupation. By the end of the first week, despite a coat that had lost all of its former sheen, despite his generally impoverished condition and a swollen and festering right front paw, he had made some small progress. Young pigs could be had with relatively little effort, for their skill at escaping was no better than his at attacking, and his desperation proved to be the more determined. Adult boars, however, were well beyond his capabilities, at least for the moment. Fox dens could be dug out, although that would be an easier task without one front paw out of commission, and the smooth otter, although a furious bundle of violent energy, could be surprised and pinned on the bank of a stream if first allowed to engage in a few of his games without disturbance and thus given the impression that all was well.

And so, hour by hour, day by day, Sarang went about repairing the almost fatal damage the love of his human friends had done him. It was a monumental accomplishment. More than once his condition became critical. Whether or not he would survive at all was often highly problematical. Had Pamela seen him during those first weeks she would not have recognized him, for he rapidly lost almost a full third of his weight. Had she recognized him, she would have despaired for his life. Why he did not return to the village where he had always known comfort, security, and a ready supply of food is something no one can answer, least of all Sarang himself, for no matter how fanciful we might wish to become about his intelligence, he never came close to the ability to reflect on his own actions. He was a cat, a wild kind of cat, nothing more, and like all of his kind he had to find a balanced relationship with his environment or perish. In time he found it.

Sarang had been gone nearly six weeks when they first heard it. It was shortly after dark and Pamela and Khoka had been put to bed. They slept on opposite sides of the thin wall that separated their rooms. Khoka heard it first.

"Paamela? Are you asleep? Did you hear that?"

"I think I heard something. Shh, there it is again!"

The sound, although from far off, from beyond the farthest field near where the *pilkhana* had once been, was clear. It rolled across the paddy fields and tumbled against the walls of the lodge. *Ah-ooo-unghhh. Aaah-oooo-unk.* It sounded like the moaning of a giant organ in a ghostly cathedral. It came again, stronger this time. *Aaah-ooooo-unghhh*. Near the edge of the forest, back in a dark little hollow, Sarang stood. He sucked his breath in sharply, dropped his bottom jaw and blew the lungfuls of air against the roof of his mouth. As he began to run out of air he moved his tongue up and slowly closed his bottom jaw, creating the sound no man can ever forget once he has heard it, the roar of a tiger in the night.

Sarang's serenade continued for fully fifteen minutes. In that time the children did not speak, or even move, for they knew the message was for them.

In the living room Liz and Glenn, too, heard Sarang call. They sat forward in their chairs, looking at each other, and listening intently.

In huts throughout the village people roused themselves on their cots and woke those who slept nearby. In the paddy field near the lodge, where the elephants were tethered, Begam Bahar, Sikander and Meernah Prue flapped their ears nervously and coiled and uncoiled their trunks. In the forest south of the village a leopard broke off his stalking of a stray goat and spat furiously into the night before slinking away, coughing and grunting to himself.

Aah-ooooo-unghhh, aah-oo-unk went the barely variable song. And then there was silence, a silence more profound than one is apt to hear in the vicinity of a jungle except in the moments after a tiger has spoken, when the desire of every living creature is to attract as little attention to itself as possible. A tiger in the night inspires anonymity as few other forces can.

"Khoka, that was Sarang. I know it was."

"*Hae,* Sarang. He has told us that all is well."

In the living room Glenn sank back in his chair. Liz heard him sigh.

"Thank God, he made it! I'll go to bed tonight for the first time in a month and a half without feeling guilty."

"Didn't you think he would?"

"Not in a million years. How did he learn to hunt? I thought for sure we killed him that day when we sent the kids away with him. I really thought we had murdered him. I can't begin to tell you what that sound does for me."

Liz, to whom it had never occurred that Sarang might not have been able to fend for himself, felt belatedly guilty.

The serenade finally ended. But the children sat motionless, still listening as the scops owl reclaimed the night.

"Paamela? What are you doing?"

"Thinking."

"Me too, Paamela. Do you think the Miracle has to do with Sarang?"

Pamela thought about it for a minute because it

was a very logical question, and a very important one.

"No, Khoka, I don't think so, because the *Shadhoobaba* told us to send him away. I don't think it's to do with Sarang. Good night, Khoka. Pleasant dreams."

19

The Trouble with Sikander

Once it was over and there was time to think it through, hindsight suggested signs that might have helped them avoid the tragedy. Ma, as the senior *mahout*, had been given Begam Bahar. It had been his choice and the only one, really, that could have been expected, since she was a *koomeriah*. Kala, as the junior man, was left with Sikander. The *makhna* seemed no less tractable than the young cow, and no one had seen any reason to question the arrangement. As a fodder-gatherer, Kala had spent years around elephants and the only reason he hadn't achieved *mahout* status before was that there had been no elephant available for him to drive.

Since most of the work was light the elephants were seldom worked together. Each morning the three *mahouts* were told what was expected of them and they would go off to collect their mounts and separate. Ma and Chooni, then, did not know that Kala was having trouble with the male, nor did anyone else. They did notice that the less experienced man was becoming more and more nervous as time went on, but no one thought to associate it with his relationship with Sikander. He was known to have had trouble with his wife on a number of occasions and his jumpiness was tacitly laid to that.

Later on, when they had an opportunity to examine Sikander, they found marks on the upper part of his trunk and along his massive shoulders. Only then, too late to do any good, did they realize that Kala had been beating his mount, presumably for being stubborn or intractable. It seemed certain, too, that he was frightened of the elephant and was mastering his fear by mastering the animal with brute force and unnecessary cruelty. It is not an unknown phenomenon among elephant men.

Glenn, of course, blamed himself. In his own mind Ata accepted the guilt, and both Manik and Masu walked around for days feeling that they had not offered the stranger from America sufficient guidance. In fact it was no one's fault. There is nothing at all unusual about an elephant turning on his *mahout* and killing him.

Just when Sikander decided that he had had enough is not easy to say. Perhaps it is exaggerating his capacities to assume that he ever made up his mind at all. Perhaps it was a reflex growing out of the conditioning the misguided Kala had been giving him.

It was just after eleven in the morning. Kala had been working Sikander south of the village, pulling out some roots in a new field that was being developed. The trees had been cut the week before and for two days the *makhna* had worked to get the logs down to the river. Now there were the roots, and it was heavy work, heavy enough, in fact, to have justified a request for assistance. A more experienced *mahout* would have sensed that he was overworking his elephant and would have waited for a second animal to be brought in. But Kala, with something to prove, worked Sikander to the limit, and the *ankus* was laid on with little restraint.

Sikander accomplished all that had been asked of him and dutifully raised his leg, allowing the freely sweating *mahout* to step off his neck. As the leg was lowered, Kala jumped to the ground and turned his back on his elephant.

Surely, at some point, Kala knew that he was about to die, but the pain could not have lasted very long. When Glenn, Ata, Manik, Masu and Ma came running down the dike in answer to the screams of

Kala's wife and the wailing that echoed throughout the village, it was all over. Tsibi had been taking lunch to her husband and arrived at the edge of the field just as Sikander struck. It was several days before she could describe it to Masu, who sat alone with her in her darkened hut not far from the riverbank.

As Kala turned his back on Sikander, the elephant seized him around the neck and flipped him upside down. It required practically no effort on Sikander's part, for Kala was a little man, weighing no more than a hundred and twenty-five pounds. Since his full weight was pivoted on his neck, it is likely that his neck was broken instantly and that he died then, before Sikander's systematic mutilation of his body.

The elephant didn't make a sound but Kala's body, as it was slammed to the ground, made a sickening thud, clearly audible to Tsibi, a hundred feet away. Sikander brought his foot down on the *mahout's* head and, using his trunk, pulled both arms out of their sockets and threw them back over his shoulder. He then walked across the body, bringing two feet down squarely on its midsection before moving off to the edge of the field where he stopped and stood under a large tree, humming and grumbling to himself. The act had been cold, calculating and efficient, accomplished with remarkable economy of movement. Although anger or resentment may have been the root cause, the deed itself was accomplished as if it were just one more little job to be done.

Glenn didn't have to move down off the dike to see what had happened. While the others ran toward Kala's wife, who was by now hysterical, he turned and raced back to the lodge. He arrived back on the scene ten minutes later, completely out of breath, carrying his .300 Magnum and a box of shells. Sikander was still standing quietly under the tree, enjoying its pleasant shade.

Jumping down into the field Glenn worked his way around the stumps and root holes to where the others were standing. Masu had already taken Kala's wife away. His hands shaking so badly that he could hardly handle the cartridges, Glenn began loading the rifle. He kept his eyes on the elephant, half expecting a charge at any moment. Ata hurried over to him and put a restraining hand on his arm.

"No, Glenn, don't."

"What the hell do you mean, 'don't.' "

Glenn realized that he was shouting but it was beyond his control. The remains of the *mahout* were literally splattered all around him and he felt himself becoming more nauseated by the minute.

"You don't have to kill him."

"What do we do, give him a medal and feed him pineapples! He's a killer!"

Again he was shouting and he realized that the others were staring at him. He looked toward the elephant and saw that Ma was quietly approaching him, *ankus* in hand. Glenn held his breath as the ex-

perienced handler commanded the elephant to turn
and to provide a leg so that he could mount. Without hesitation Sikander responded to the commands
he knew so well and Ma positioned himself on his
neck and began moving him around the field and
down toward the river.

"It's not done that way here, Glenn. Whatever happened, it was the *mahout's* fault. The elephant is not
to blame and he must not be killed."

"You mean . . . you just let bygones be bygones?
You just kiss and make up? I don't believe it!"

Villagers were arriving with sheets with which they
would remove Kala's remains. As they moved mourn-
fully along the dike Ata took Glenn's arm and led
him away. Glenn felt ill, physically and mentally.

"Glenn, you must understand these things. When a
man decides to become a *mahout* he knows what can
happen to him if he misjudges his animal. The elephant is never wrong. Sikander can still give years of
good service and probably will never turn again."

"But what if he does?"

"Then he will get a third *mahout* who will profit
from the mistakes of the other two. An animal can
be misjudged, Glenn, mishandled, but he can't be
wrong. Only men can be wrong. We have taken the
elephant from the forest and made him work for us.
He has tried to learn, tried to please us, and we must
not kill him for a failure of our own.

They were sitting on the dike facing into the adjoining field. Glenn was shaking his head, trying to comprehend Ata's logic, so totally incompatible with everything he had ever known or believed. He had read of an elephant in the San Francisco Zoo that had turned and killed its keeper. It was shot that same night by a squad of police with high-powered rifles. And now this. It seemed illogical and cruel, cruel to the memory of the man who had just been torn apart and cruel to his replacement, who would take the same risks.

"That's a hell of a philosophy, Ata!"

"Don't you have industrial accidents in your country?"

"Well, sure we do."

"Do you throw the machine away?"

Somehow this made sense, but then again it didn't. Glenn still had the urge to run after the elephant and gun it down, destroy it for what it had done. But that didn't make sense either, for that was merely vengeance. Ma now had Sikander under control, that was obvious. Ma would now take him and the more docile Begam Bahar would go to Kala's replacement, if one could be found.

The replacement was found. There is always a line-up of prospective *mahouts* in every village, waiting for an opportunity to get a mount. By the strangest of coincidences Kala's replacement, a handsome, lithe nineteen-year-old youth, bore the same name. Ever after, when Glenn would call him or refer to him, his blood would run cold and a little bit of his original rage would return. But Glenn was in elephant country, working within the framework of the elephant tradition. This, the death and dismemberment of a man, was a part of it. And this Glenn had to learn to accept.

In time, the ugly episode became a memory, albeit a bad one, but nothing more.

True to Ata's prediction, Sikander was returned to the fields and performed flawlessly under Ma's expert handling. Ata would later declare that Glenn's understanding of this, his gradual acceptance of it, perhaps more than anything else made him a part of the elephant tradition. This horror of which he had been a part was the initiation fee Glenn had to pay, he would later reflect. It seemed small compared to Kala's. In his entire life he had worked only sixty-one days as a *mahout*, the job that had been his ambition since childhood. He had worked as a fodder-gatherer for thirteen long years while waiting for his opportunity.

Although Khoka's relationship with the discernible universe was defined through the traditions of Buddhism, his life had been spent too close to the jungle's edge and the forces that shaped Hindu philosophy for him to be free of the mysticism for which the Subcontinent is so well known. Omens, signs and small protective devices were all a part of his existence.

The small harmless threads of primitivism that ran through the fabric of his life were not really religious in nature, but there was an essence of predetermination about them. The more he sought for his Miracle the more important those threads became. Unfortunately, there were times when Pamela couldn't keep up with him. Compared with Khoka, Pamela, the dreamer, the sentimentalist, was wholly pragmatic.

There had been a touch of the theosophical about their meeting with the *Shadhoobaba*, at least to Khoka's mind. Before Sarang led them to him — and Khoka was firmly convinced that Sarang had done just that — the existence of the hermit was no more a demonstrable fact than the existence of any magical personage Khoka might wish to conjure up. The fact that Sarang had been sent to him temporarily, as had now proven to be the case, so that he could find the *Shadhoobaba*, who in turn could tell him how to regain his sight, seemed to fit into some still vague cause and effect relationship. Prince had been a link, a kind of living sacrifice who had come from across the sea to start the chain of events in motion. It wasn't an easy picture for Khoka to paint, but a person living in total and perpetual darkness, even a little boy, has a lot of time to think. One either enriches his internal life or perishes emotionally in such a situation. He hadn't yet been able to establish Pamela's connection with all this, although it was plain that she had come before Prince and might therefore be considered the legitimate first link. But then there was Liz, on whom Khoka was becoming increasingly dependent. In the biological sense she had come before Pamela, but at about that point Khoka's otherwise reasonably clear picture of the whole mystic association began to fog. He tried to explain it to Pamela but she never was quite able to grasp it. And it wasn't a language barrier that stood between them. It was something far more profound than that.

The more intent he became on locating and executing his Miracle the less tolerance Khoka had for the loose ends that still taunted him when he tried to think the whole thing through. Although he was not equipped to intellectualize about it, his approach was essentially Eastern. He tried to draw the mental circles that would encompass the whole and show that each event and each personality was the product of all the others and that each was inevitably bringing him closer to the climactic moment when the miraculous would be done and the veil would lift from his eyes. He wasn't the least embarrassed by the idea that he seemed to be at the center of it all, and didn't bother to expand his philosophical geometry so that the center of one circle would be nothing but a point on the circumference of another.

Shortly after their return to the village Pamela tried to find a niche in her concept of Christianity that could logically accommodate the *Shadhoobaba*.

It wasn't an easy task and she frightened herself away from the project when she found herself wondering if the old man could possibly be Christ reborn. She was certain that that thought was terribly and even dangerously wrong, so she began looking for more profitable avenues with fewer inherent hazards. She never even tried to discuss it with Khoka. She was sure that his reply would only compound her confusion.

Although neither child had been raised in a particularly religious home and neither had a firm grasp of any ordered system of metaphysical belief, the inevitable outcome of their individual reflections was a kind of united ecstasy. They were apart only in the details; in spirit they were together. They began sharing more and more secrets, and Liz was troubled by the amount of whispering that went on. The outcome of their last secret plan was only too fresh in her memory. She reflected, too, that Pamela had never been a secretive child and it troubled her to see a change coming over her. Growing pains, she told herself a number of times, just growing pains. After all, she mused, she is going to be a teen-ager soon. But Liz never quite convinced herself and continued to worry.

Glenn had very definite guilt feelings about the ruse involving the *Shadhoobaba* and sought no opportunities to reflect on the matter. He somehow associated Liz's misgivings with the calculated deceit and did his best to banish the whole thing from his mind. He felt that he would have to face an accusing daughter eventually and anything he could do to avoid that confrontation was automatically a preferred course of action.

Viewed in combination or individually, neither Pamela nor Khoka could be accused of deviousness. They did not wish to operate outside of the family unit and they did not plan any further escapades. Their whispered secrets were nothing more than the comparing of notes and the exchange of views on commonplace happenings. They were simply seeking the Miracle in everything they saw and heard. While they had not yet become exactly obsessive on the subject they were decidedly mystic and in the end it amounted to somewhat the same thing.

Khoka was still convinced that the Miracle centered on Sarang. He didn't know how it would manifest itself but time and again he told Pamela that Sarang would be involved. His feelings in this regard were even stronger on those nights when Sarang came to the edge of the field and called. Both children tried to divine some message in the regularity of the concerts and Pamela began keeping a calendar. It hung in her bedroom and was labeled, very simply, "Sarang's Visits." It worked out that the tiger came to the outskirts of the village and called every fifth evening. It was so regular an event that Khoka began to look for a mystic value in the number five. Even

Pamela began to think there might be something to it.

Although neither Pamela nor Khoka had access to the information, the number five has been invested with magical powers at different times and in different places throughout recorded history. To Pythagoras, who theorized that numbers contained the basic elements of all things natural and spiritual, the number five was the divisor of ten, which was the sum total of all numbers. Five became, then, the number for justice. Elsewhere it had been noted that five was the number of senses with which a whole man is endowed (this might have been readily siezed upon by Khoka if he had been familiar with the concept); the wounds of Christ were five; and the name of the Deity, the Pentagram, contained five letters. None of this Khoka knew. Somewhere, though, he had heard that in the scale of magical numbers, five provided protection against wild beasts. Perhaps it is not surprising that Khoka should have thought this, for the protective value of certain numbers has always been a widespread belief in widely divergent cultures.

Actually, there was nothing at all mystical about Sarang's appearance every fifth night. He was still having a great deal of trouble feeding himself and he had established a large hunting range, or block, that he patrolled endlessly in search of easy prey. Fortunately for him, tigers are now rare enough in the

Chittagong Hill Tracts so that he was able to claim much more territory than a normal tiger needs or indeed would find available in better populated tiger country. He drove out a young clouded leopard and killed a golden cat. The sounds of the battle echoed throughout the forest for fully ten minutes before the small but no less fierce feline lay dead at his feet. It had been a mature animal and what it lacked in size it made up for in speed and experienced fighting skill. Sarang would carry the scars of that battle with him as long as he lived. His wounds were open and bleeding freely while he ate the cat. There was another tiger in the area, a rather sedate old male, but the territory was big enough so that they never clashed.

With the lesser cats gone from the area, Sarang established an equilibrium with the other tiger's habits and was free to patrol his block at leisure. He was unable to kill larger animals because their experience in jungle survival made them far too elusive. On the two occasions when he had managed to get close enough to rush adult sambars, he didn't know where to grab them for a sure kill. The mutilated stags were able to break his grip and escape. Although desperately hungry, on the one occasion when he successfully stalked a mature boar, he was outbluffed and driven off. The five-hundred-pound animal made his determination to stay alive appear particularly convincing by displaying eleven-inch tusks, well wetted with saliva and ready for blood. Sarang was forced to rely on immature animals and those which had no adequate defenses. Sad to relate, he did not know how to kill even these without a great deal more butchery than was required. His victims suffered needlessly and his feeding was the occasion for a great deal more distressing noise than is usually the case with tigers who have learned their predatory arts well.

Because he did require a constant food supply and because his prey had to be immature, his roaming was constant. He established a regular route and through the simple geography of his range arrived at the outskirts of Pukmaranpur every fifth day.

To say that Sarang missed his old friends or longed to be with them would be to endow him with emotional equipment he did not have. Still, Pukmaranpur held memories for him, at least memories of good feelings, if not of specific events. He was drawn to the area and would have remained there if the food supply had been reliable. His inexperience, though, condemned him to wander, and the closest he came to reaching out for some part of what he had lost was his serenading near the edge of the old *pilkhana*.

The fact that the tiger called every fifth night had not escaped the notice of the other inhabitants of the village. Liz and Glenn, the elders, and even the children of the village learned to wait for the first deep *aah-ooo-unghhh* that inevitably came within half an hour after sundown. When the last sliver of red showed above the trees to the west, the villagers would sit and wait. In time, the day when Sarang's visit was due became known as the *Day of the Tiger* and things were reckoned from it. At first his original detractors took advantage of Satwyne's absence from the village to begin talking of the threat the tiger obviously still represented. Most of the villagers, though, had had enough of the old trouble and popular apathy brought the matter to an end. Sarang's concerts were suffered in silence. Before long they became a normal part of the lives of the villagers. The visits were rather more than that for Pamela and Khoka, though, and both Glenn and Liz realized that they would eventually have to face the prospect of a reunion.

Liz found it much easier to be strict with Pamela than with Khoka. Her hold on the boy was still provisional and she was quite understandably reluctant to be severe with him. Recognizing this as a clearly evident fact of life, the children decided that Khoka should be the one to ask Liz to intercede with Glenn on their behalf. Khoka posed the question the morning after a particularly long and melodious solo by Sarang.

Liz didn't know how to evaluate the request, for she felt the answer should rest on one factor only: would Sarang now be dangerous? After the children had gone to bed that night she hesitantly laid the matter before Glenn. His first reaction was explosive. To him it represented the potential rebirth of the thorniest single problem he had faced since arriving at the village. He was not at all receptive to anything that might result in the necessity of his facing it again. As the evening wore on, however, he relented and agreed to discuss the matter with an open mind. He agreed as well that the only factor to be considered was the safety of the children. He had known Sarang too long and seen him play with the children too often to believe in his heart that he would ever hurt them. Reluctantly, Glenn agreed that before sunset on the next *Day of the Tiger* he would accompany the two children to the field beyond the old *pilkhana* and see if Sarang cared to show himself. He didn't feel it necessary to mention the fact that he would be armed.

On the morning of the fifth day both Khoka and Pamela awoke earlier than usual. The last owls were winging their way across the paddy fields toward their daytime roosts at the edge of the forest when Pamela heard Khoka rapping softly on the wall. She had been awake for a quarter of an hour listening to the metallic, grating mew of two peacocks that had stationed themselves on parallel dikes and were competing for the attention of the sun.

"I'm awake, Khoka."

"I can hear the peacock. It must be *sokal baela*."

"It is. I can see the sun."

"It is *baghh din*, Paamela."

"*Hae,* Khoka, it is the *Day of the Tiger.*"

Both children had resigned themselves to the fact that Glenn would accompany them when they sought to reestablish contact with their former pet. When he hadn't come in from the fields by three o'clock Pamela thought she would burst with impatience. They sat with Liz on the veranda sipping the tea that Raanaa had brought them with a platter of rice flour cookies and a sliced mango.

"Do you think he's forgotten, Mummy?"

"No, honey, I don't. And you don't either. He gave you his word. It's only three and he said by three-thirty."

The last half hour dragged on interminably but Glenn arrived at the last minute and went into the lodge. When he came back outside Pamela and Khoka were standing at the foot of the steps, marking time. Pamela froze when she saw that he was carrying his rifle but said nothing out of respect for Khoka's feelings. She looked at her father questioningly but he just raised his eyebrows slightly and nodded to her. Why can't they ever understand, she thought, why can't they ever *believe*?

They arrived at the site of the old *pilkhana* just after four o'clock. It was still hot and they found their old shade tree, where they settled down to wait. They could not be sure that Sarang was even in the area. They had never heard him before sundown, and that was still hours away.

But Sarang was in the area and had been since early morning. He had managed to take a peacock shortly before dawn and had bedded down not far from the edge of the forest. Although Glenn and the children were hidden by the thick trunk of the banyan tree he knew they were there and was on his feet, moving along the forest front beyond the first line of brush. He stopped several times, uncertain of what to do, and finally lowered his head and snorted. Several more times he exhaled explosively and made a quick series of soft *ungh-ungh-ungh* sounds. Pamela was on her feet at the first snort with Khoka right behind her. Glenn cautioned them to wait to see what would happen. Out of Pamela's line of sight he slipped the safety off his Magnum.

Again Sarang snorted and made several grunting sounds. Pamela was unable to locate him in the thick brush and stood her ground, calling softly. Khoka reached out to take her arm and stepped forward until he was abreast of her. He called Sarang in the way he always had, repeating *baghh baghh baghh* very rapidly, puffing his cheeks up with each pronunciation so that the sound had something of a hen's clucking about it. Before he could repeat the call a second time the bushes parted and Sarang's forequarters emerged, deep-orange in the late afternoon sun.

Pamela had the almost uncontrollable urge to run forward and throw herself on his neck as she had so many times in the past, but she was aware of her father right behind her and knew that a precipitous act on her part might spell disaster. She walked forward slowly, taking Khoka's hand in her own. Glenn moved off slightly to the side so that the children wouldn't be between his rifle and the tiger. Sarang appeared to be very much bigger than Glenn remembered him, and he was having qualms. He was about to call the children back when Sarang stepped out of the brush, sat down and yawned mightily with the same *ow-wow-wow* sound he had always made.

The children continued to move steadily forward, with Glenn moving on a parallel course, his rifle at the ready. When no more than fifty feet separated them, he called to the children, "Wait there and see what he does. Don't move any closer. If he still wants to be friends he'll come to you."

Khoka dropped to his knees and repeated his soft, hen-like *baghh baghh baghh* call. Before Glenn could react, Sarang was bounding toward the children. By the time he had his rifle to his shoulder Sarang was upon them. He bowled Pamela right off her feet and was pawing Khoka's hands, trying to get them away from his face — an old game of theirs. As Khoka dropped his hands and threw his head back the rough tongue of the tiger found its mark. Both children were laughing uncontrollably.

Glenn sat in the grass about twenty feet off and watched. The gun seemed so silly and overly dramatic now that he slipped the safety back on and pushed it away where he wouldn't have to look at it. For forty-five minutes he watched the children and the tiger play. Sarang was no different from what he had always been. He never showed any inclination to bring either his teeth or his claws into play, no matter how rough it became. That's more than I could say for some house cats I've known, Glenn thought, and felt even more foolish about the rifle.

After they had tumbled together and after Sarang had thoroughly soaked them with his endless licking they moved over under the tree where they had spent their last hours together. Sarang stretched out between them as he had always done and Pamela began examining his coat. If anything his fur was a little more wiry than it had been before and he seemed a little darker. But it was Khoka's inquiring fingers that first found the scars suffered in the battle with the golden cat and Pamela chided him for his battle wounds.

When Glenn finally joined them under the tree Sarang responded by rolling over on his back and extending his front paws upward. Glenn pressed down on his pads as he had done so many times in the past while Sarang pushed back in a rocking motion, moving one leg up, and then the other. As Glenn knelt beside him to scratch him under the chin, Sarang began his purring sounds.

"What do you think of him now, Daddy?"

Glenn smiled at Pamela.

"He's a little bigger and an awful lot wiser, I'll bet, but he's the same monster he always was. Why, what do you think of him?"

Pamela responded by throwing herself across Sarang's chest and hugging him with all her might. Sarang snorted once and laid his great paw across her shoulders. Khoka sat at his head, running his hands over his face, rediscovering the details that were as familiar to him as his own body.

"Glennsaheb?"

"Yes, Khoka?"

"Is this a Miracle?"

Pamela heard the question and buried her face deeper into Sarang's neck. *He's going to give it away,* she thought, *he's going to give it away!*

"Yes, Khoka, I guess it is. I think all love is a Miracle."

And that was as far as the conversation went.

Glenn let the children remain with Sarang until the last minute. Once again Sarang allowed them to leave without attempting to follow. When they had gone about fifty feet, Pamela turned to look. Sarang was standing beneath the tree, looking after them. As she watched he turned slowly and walked off toward the brush. It seemed to her that his stride was stronger, more assured than when he had lived with them in the village. Despite his size he was liquid in his movements, each motion flowing naturally into the next. It seemed to her that she had never seen anything more beautiful in her life.

As they walked back to the village Pamela moved ahead with Khoka. She was anxious that her father not see the tears in her eyes.

"Did you notice, Khoka, he still wore the necklace!"

"Of course, Paamela. The bracelet made him king. It wouldn't be Sarang without the bracelet. He will never lose that!"

20

The Cave

The next three times Sarang's hunting cycle brought him to the vicinity of Pukmaranpur, Pamela and Khoka were there to meet him, with Glenn in attendance at a discreet distance. On the last of the three occasions Liz was there too, for Glenn had suggested that it would now be safe for the children to go alone and Liz wanted to see for herself. It wasn't that she distrusted Glenn's judgment, but sending one's children off to the edge of the jungle to rendezvous with a wild tiger has certain emotional overtones. Liz found that she needed more than an abstract intellectual understanding of it to be able to live with the idea.

The eccentric nature of the situation forcibly impressed itself on Liz a few days later when she tried to explain it in a letter to her sister. She and Glenn were sitting on the veranda later that night, as they did every night before retiring, trying to work it all out in her mind.

"You know, I couldn't find a way to explain it to Kip. It's just too weird. People would think we were crazy. I don't know, maybe we are!"

"I don't think we are, and neither do you. Don't ever try to explain Sarang to anyone because it can't be done. He doesn't fit into any normal pattern. He's one of those screwy things that just happen."

"I guess so. Just as long as the kids are safe. That's all I care about."

Glenn thought carefully before he answered. The next day was Sarang's day and would mark the first time the children would be allowed to go to him alone. The fact that Liz had brought up the subject and expressed even the beginnings of a doubt shifted the responsibility to him.

"They'll be safe."

Several times during the course of the day Liz reviewed with the children the conditions under which permission had been granted. They were to do as they had done on the four other occasions when they had gone to meet Sarang with Glenn in attendance. They were not to approach the forest under any conditions. They were to wait by the banyan tree and call. If Sarang did not come to them exactly as he had in the past, they were to return home immediately. Pamela was to wear her mother's watch and be back at the lodge exactly two hours from the moment they left. They were not to lead Sarang out of the *pilkhana* area and not to coax him if he didn't come to them willingly.

The children did not find the conditions oppressive and readily agreed to all of them. They wanted only to see Sarang again and be alone with him. Their time alone with Sarang, all the time they had known in the past and now would know again, had very special meanings for both Pamela and Khoka. His presence had the effect of lowering a curtain that shut out a world that was at once demanding and harsh. Sarang was a living fantasy, and he enabled them to enter into a world of make-believe the likes of which a normally situated child could seek only in dreams. The great striped rectangle of a cat was a fairy tale come to life, a lie that was truth, a denial of adult reality and social norm. Every child devises such creatures in his dreams. Pamela and Khoka could hug theirs and feel his warmth and his responsiveness. Their consuming desire to be with him alone again was a hunger for what they were both in the process of losing. They were growing up, and Sarang represented what was being taken away from them. The inexorability of growth, while beautiful as it opens new doors and brings new rewards, can also be burdensome for those caught on the horns of transition. It was that time of life for both Pamela and Khoka. They were approaching twelve and the time was not too distant when even their feelings about each other would begin to change. Sarang, then, was more than a pet or an old friend. He was pivotal, a talisman, a last hold on something they were about to abandon — their childhood.

A dry coughing grunt greeted them as they approached the banyan tree and Khoka went to his knees for his greeting ritual. *Baghh baghh baghh* he clucked in explosive little sounds, *baghh baghh baghh*. Cautiously, as he had now learned to approach all situations, Sarang showed himself in front of the same bush he always used. *Baghh baghh baghh*, Khoka called again and Sarang was at their sides nuzzling them, pawing them carefully with his now devastatingly sharp claws well sheathed, and rasping them with his saw blade tongue until they were hopelessly wet and helpless with giggling.

For a little over an hour they belonged to that world to which Sarang was the key. Pamela was very much aware of the fact that their demeanor this time would govern the amount of latitude they would have in the future so she kept a careful check on the time. All too soon and with agonizing reluctance she told Khoka they had to go. They left Sarang as they had on five other occasions, alone by the tree. Somehow, though, it wasn't sad anymore. Now their leaving was nothing more than an interruption, for the relationship had been successfully restructured. They no longer had a tiger cub for a pet, but something even better, something even more wonderfully outrageous: they had a wild tiger for a friend. In another way it was better too, for the anticipation of seeing him again enabled them to bound forward through time in five-day intervals. It was a game of leapfrog with the calendar.

Satwyne's return from upriver was eagerly awaited by Khoka. Although he loved being with Liz, and particularly with Pamela, Khoka adored his father, whom he was sure was the bravest of men. His return was unannounced and the first Khoka knew of it was when Bolo Bahadur's trunk came snaking through the lodge window to snatch a rice cooky out of his hand. Pamela had watched Satwyne silently positioning the big *koonki* outside the window and had given herself a stomach-ache struggling to repress her laughter. Khoka spun around in his chair and felt along the rough trunk as it came back through the window seeking new prizes. He knew from the familiar ridges and creases that it was his father's beloved *koonki*.

"*Baba! Baba!*" he cried as he ran across the fa-

273

miliar room and down the veranda steps. As he reached the *koonki* he grasped the right front leg and rode up with it, all the while shimmying forward as if he were on an inclined branch of a tree. His father's hand was outstretched and waiting. Bolo Bahadur saluted the lodge with upraised trunk, backed, turned, and headed for home.

That night Khoka lay awake for hours trying to re-create the mental pictures his father had drawn for him of the big *mela shikar* operation in which he had taken part. Five fine animals had been taken by two teams in just under two weeks of actual hunting. It had taken them several weeks, however, to get the herd in position so that they could move in.

But a pall had hung over the hunt for Sabal Kali had not been involved in it. Shortly after leaving Pukmaranpur the *koonki* had been attacked by a lone tusker in *musth*. The charge had been so sudden and so violent that the cow had panicked momentarily. Oroon, Rauton and Khada had been unable to duck low enough as the cow pushed under an enormous, sagging branch beside the trail. All three men had been swept off her back, falling onto the trail just in front of the enraged tusker. It had been impossible to identify their bodies and only when Sabal Kali showed up in a nearby village where she was known was it possible to make the association between the once great *bor phandi* and his crew and the mutilated remains that had been buried in three shallow graves heaped high with stones.

Every village in the world has its peculiar legends centering on former inhabitants. In the West the object of the legend is usually a haunted house where, very often, it is rumored that a madwoman once burned her children or butchered her husband or kept prisoners in her attic. In the East the tales often revolve around a vanished race of people, for there history has been longer in the making. Pukmaranpur was no exception.

Khoka, because he had been forced by fate to become a listener, had absorbed most of the stories that had been told of the village's unknown past. He was a kind of walking catalog, quick to make associations between new experiences and old tales. The *mondir* and the *Shadhoobaba* who lived there had been one such story.

The cave was another.

It had been rumored for uncounted generations that within the confines of the village there was a giant cave, although its whereabouts was unknown. There were different stories concerning the cave. In one it was a place of hidden treasure; in another, a temple where human sacrifices had been made to a long forgotten god who ruled harshly before the advent of gentle Buddha.

Khoka had no opinion as to what the cave had been used for, but he did believe in its existence. Since he hadn't been having any luck locating his Miracle in the everyday life within the village, he began to look for the richer fields more imaginative tales seemed to promise. Pursuit of one such tale had set him on the right road and it seemed perfectly logical that the pursuit of another might enable him to locate his goal.

"But, Khoka, we promised not to do anything like that again. We gave our word!"

"Ah, Paamela. *Na, na, na!* We promised not to go to the forest. We promised to stay in the village and the cave is here, somewhere in the village."

Pamela remembered the conversation very well and recalled almost the exact words that had been used. *"There is enough for you to explore right here in Pukmaranpur,"* her mother had said, *"and you don't have to go off in the jungle where you can get into trouble."* As she sat looking at Khoka, Pamela searched her soul. She really was determined not to put her parents through another severe trial.

"All right, Khoka, I'll help you find it, but it has to be here in the village. I don't know what it has to do with your Miracle but at least we can find out where it is."

Satwyne wasn't very much help although he did admit that as a child he had heard about the mysterious cave and had believed in it. However, he hastened to add, no one now alive knew where it was. Pamela tried Ata on the subject. He smiled somewhat patronizingly, she thought, and told her that he hadn't been raised in the village and didn't know anything about it. But, he added, his own village was over two hundred miles away and it had a legend about a cave, too.

"All villages have such stories, Pamela. They are almost never true. People accept them and pass them along to make up for the fact that there are no written records. Because the real histories of these villages are lost, these stories appear. They give the people a feeling of belonging to something old and important, even if it is unknown."

Pamela, who had watched Ata guide her father so wisely and so well when they first arrived in the village, had a great deal of respect for him. She went to Khoka with Ata's explanation. Khoka rejected it firmly and completely.

"What would he have said if you had asked him about the *Shadhoobaba?*"

Pamela had to admit that his answer would no doubt have been the same. And so she agreed again to help Khoka find the cave.

It seemed logical to both children that the entrance to the cave would not be on flat ground. That limited the search to five places: the four hills and the steep river bank. The river bank, although they paid it a few visits, was ruled out almost at the outset. It was one of the most heavily trafficked areas in all of Pukmaranpur and had long since been deprived of all cover. A dozen pathways led down its face and where it was too steep, steps had been cut, giving access to the narrow shelf that ran along just inches above water level. Then, too, Pamela pointed out, almost all of the bank was visible from the river, and hundreds of fishermen had come and gone without reporting a cave opening. It was to the four hills that they must look.

The lower slopes of three of the hills had been under cultivation for generations and didn't seem likely to hold many secrets. The tops of two of the hills held clusters of huts and had been playgrounds for the children who lived there for as far back as anyone could remember. The third hill had long ago been cleared and every inch of it was known to the village's children. It was highly unlikely, they reasoned, that hundreds of children, pursuing each other and hiding from each other down through the years in their endless games, would not have turned something up, if there was anything there.

Their reasoning was valid and they turned their attention to the fourth hill, the hill on which the Buddhist temple stood. The temple itself was quite obviously the oldest building in Pukmaranpur and nothing in the way of construction had been done on either the slopes or the crown of the hill within the memory of living man. Then, too, Pamela observed, as they sat studying the hill, all traffic to and from the temple was by way of the fifty-two stone steps that ran straight up the eastern slope from the dike below. No children ran screaming down its sides and no plows furrowed its sharply sloping faces. It seemed quite clear to them that the cave must be in the most obvious place of all, on the high ground that was at once the geological, architectural and spiritual center of Pukmaranpur.

"But, would they tell us anything, Khoka? I don't think they would."

Pamela was referring to the two monks who lived within the confines of the shrine. Khoka was urging a visit to them. He reasoned that they were the only ones who really knew anything about the hill. No one else ever went there except by way of the steps and a visit to the shrine by the devout wasn't exactly a trip of exploration. The hill and all that it might contain were the sole province of the two men who lived there, one very old, which in itself was promising, and one very young.

Pamela had never been up this hill, for she had received a stern lecture on respecting other people's religions before they arrived in the village. To her it seemed to represent something rather forbidding. But Khoka kept the issue alive, assuring her that the monks were kind men who would welcome their visit and answer their questions if they could. When Pamela still resisted, Khoka brought his ultimate weapon into play. They had not yet found his Miracle, he reminded her, so it almost certainly had to do with the cave. Sarang, while still a great joy to them for an hour every fifth day, had not proven to be the source that Khoka had originally thought he would be. Therefore, Khoka would remain blind as long as he was denied access to the cave and the secret it obviously held. His belief in the existence of the *Shadhoobaba* had started him on the road to sight; only the discovery of the cave would enable him to complete the journey. And without Pamela's help, Khoka was doomed. Ergo, only Pamela stood between him and the world of the sighted. Pamela, who found the feeling of guilt all but intolerable, buckled under the impact of his logic and agreed that on the morning of the next *din baghh* she would mount the fifty-two stone steps with Khoka and face the monks in their lair. It was decided to wait the extra two days because they were still convinced that there was a magical quality to Sarang's precisely timed visits.

Pamela's misgivings about their impending ascent to the shrine were not without basis, although this was unknown to her. There was a strict tradition at the shrine that no foreigners be permitted to enter the sacred grounds. A number of years before a very young, brash English lord had chosen to conduct a *shikar* along the Gamalbuk River on his honeymoon and had arrived with his new bride to live in the hunting lodge. While his valet and his wife's maid set about unpacking and making the lodge suitable for their residency, the young couple set out to explore the village, which was pretty much the same then as it was when the Barclays arrived. They soon found the steps to the shrine and arrived at the summit without attracting the attention of the monks who were then in residence. The senior monk came upon the young groom focusing his box camera on his bride, who was sitting in the lap of Buddha, planting a very large and noisy kiss on his lips. The elderly monk was not amused.

Even the young man's father who saw the report in his capacity as a highly placed official in the Colonial Office was able to understand the consternation of the monks. The official apologies that were circulated stopped the storm of protest that seemed about to erupt into something rather ugly, but the shrine on the high hill at Pukmaranpur had been traditionally off limits to outsiders ever since. The thoughtless insult to Buddha had long been forgotten but the tradition remained, even though it was known only to the monks who lived there.

Pamela and Khoka moved slowly along the stone path that led from the fifty-second step to the stone arch. It was the only opening in the walls that enclosed two-thirds of the hilltop. They arrived at the ancient structure to find their way blocked by the younger monk. He wasn't unfriendly and even managed to smile reassuringly at Pamela as he told her that she would have to wait outside. When Khoka explained that they hadn't really come to the shrine at all but only to ask a question, the monk stepped out and joined them on the pathway.

The young monk told them that he thought he had heard something about an ancient cave, but the old monk would be the one to know, and since he was meditating at the moment they would have to come back another time.

Twice more they climbed slowly up the long flight of steps to the top of the hill and twice more the old monk was unavailable to them. As they descended the hill for the third time something caught Pamela's attention to the right of the steps midway down the steep slope. The hill as a whole was masked with a rather uniform cover of low trees except for the steps themselves, which formed a narrow avenue from top to bottom. At the midway point the color of the vegetation changed for a distance of about ten feet and then resumed its hue of broad-leaved hunter's green. She stopped to examine the phenomenon for a moment and realized where the difference lay. For about ten feet a band of brush ran off at a right angle from the pathway. It consisted of pale apple-green bushes, the kind she had observed growing at the edge of the jungle wherever it struggled to reclaim a cleared field. It was the kind of brush Sarang always emerged from. She had learned enough from conversations in her agriculturally oriented home to know that it was secondary growth, brush that grew on ground that had once been cleared of original cover.

"Khoka. Why would there be a path around the side of the hill?"

"There wouldn't be. No one uses the hill and no one goes there except to the temple at the top."

"But, Khoka, there once was a path about halfway up the hill. I saw it on the way down. There is brush there now but it is like the brush at the edge of the forest. It isn't at all like the rest. The leaves are smaller and have a funny prickly shape instead of being big and smooth."

Khoka hummed softly to himself and looked very grave.

"Paamela, if we follow that old path we will find the cave. It would be there, for no one ever goes to that place. My Miracle is there, too."

Pamela gazed at Khoka, now utterly absorbed by this new information. It suddenly occurred to her that a circle was being drawn to a close. It somehow seemed that everything was fitting into place and that the search begun in the middle of the night so many weeks before was about to come to an end.

21

The Miracle

The expedition was put off until the following morning. Neither Pamela nor Khoka was inclined toward another escapade in the dark and it was already well past four o'clock. Since the next day was Saturday, they would not have to attend Liz's morning classes and could start out right after breakfast.

Neither of them slept very much that night. Pamela was stricken with guilt, for she was sure this was something she should discuss with her parents. Yet she knew they would forbid the search simply because the quest would take them to the hill with the shrine on top. It was an area she felt sure they would consider off limits. On the other hand, she felt she owed it to Khoka to help him locate his Miracle and regain his sight. She was enormously curious about it herself. She had never seen a Miracle and being in on the ground floor of one appealed to her sense of the dramatic. After endless soul-searching she was able to justify her final support of Khoka's quest on the technicality that it would not take them beyond the village limits and she would not be breaking any specific promise she had made.

Khoka's night, too, was largely sleepless. He sensed the end of his quest and spent most of the night planning what he would do once his sight was restored. The Miracle was something he believed in implicitly, and it still hadn't occurred to him that he might not be up to the task once he found out what it was. His belief and his faith were total. It penetrated to the very core of his consciousness and beyond. It was the kind of faith Dr. Noor had told Glenn that Khoka would have to find on his own.

Because Khoka could not consciously recall any other way of life, his blindness had not been something he worried about day and night until the advent of Pamela, Sarang and the *Shadhoobaba*. It was something he had adjusted to and he could not really imagine how it would be to live any other way. The expansion of his world through his friendship with Pamela, however, had changed all that. Now he desperately wanted to see. Most of all he wanted to know what Pamela looked like, and to see Sarang. And it was no small afterthought that he was determined to become a *phandi,* a *bor phandi* like his father. He was riding off on *shikar* on his magnificent imaginary *koonki* of the future when he finally fell asleep a couple of hours before sunrise.

While Pamela and Khoka sorted out their emotions and dreamed their dreams, other forces were at work. A widespread low pressure area that had been building up over the Bay of Bengal for days broke through a high pressure ridge that had been born in the mountains of Nepal. It began moving across the land to the north and east. The day dawned behind a sullen sky. The light was brittle and the mood threatening. The wind turned leaves over on the highest branches of the tallest trees. Birds stayed on their perches and the smaller mammals looked cautiously about before leaving their burrows.

As the children emerged from the lodge, where Khoka had been permitted to spend the night, Pamela noticed that there was an unusual amount of traffic along the dikes. Her heart sank as they neared the hill. With the wind gusting around them and with their white *lungis* in stark contrast to the blackening sky, dozens of villagers were moving slowly up the stone stairs. She could see a small crowd milling around on the flat plaza outside the archway at the top of the hill. They had not heard in the lodge that the old monk had died during the night.

"Khoka! There are hundreds, just hundreds of people on the steps and on the hill. We could never go up there today without being seen by everyone!"

She could see Khoka sag under the impact of her news. He had waited too long and was too keyed up after almost an entire night of preparation to postpone it now.

"Paamela, please! It must be today. I know it. It must be today!"

"Khoka, what can I do? The steps are crowded with people going up and coming down. Everyone would see us if we went up part way and then just vanished into the bushes. They'd know something was up."

"Then we must go up through the brush and not by the steps. No one can see us that way."

Slowly Pamela scanned the steep slopes of the hill. She had negotiated similar brush patches in the forest and could envision what her clothes would look like if she tried the ascent all the way to the swath of applegreen.

"Khoka, no one goes that way and there'll be thousands of snakes. Maybe there'll be a lot of cobras. What do we do then?"

"They won't harm us. The *Shadhoobaba* has given us this mission and he will protect us. After we find the cave, Paamela, you will never have to lead me anywhere again."

The ascent was not as difficult as Pamela had feared. They slipped into the dense, low-growing brush at the bottom of the hill without being seen and emerged under a canopy of stunted, thick-trunked trees. Although they had to keep their heads down, they were able to move up the slope without fighting through the dense tangles Pamela had anticipated with such terrible misgivings. The rise was steep but the matted debris under the trees provided good footing. Khoka received several rather painful scratches and blows when he failed to keep his head low enough but he didn't complain and Pamela was unaware of his difficulties. Their route ran parallel to the steps about twenty yards off to the left. From time to time they could hear muffled voices through the trees. The villagers wound endlessly to the shrine where the dead monk's body lay wrapped in saffron yellow.

Overhead, beyond the treetops that held the children in a secluded green world, the sky continued to toil. Millions of tons of water, divided into minute droplets, drifted northward carrying the substance of the Indian Ocean toward the mountains beyond. Far below, down the river, beyond where the great swamp marked the edge of the lake, small eddies of wind swirled menacingly shoreward, threatening the jungle with the storm that was gathering its strength.

To the west, in the harbor at Chittagong, tethered ships began rocking as the water rolled inward against the bulkheads and the blackened legs of the crowded piers. To the north and west, in Dacca, shopkeepers began moving perishable wares inside, abandoning the thronged sidewalks where so much of their business was done.

Their exertions kept the children from appreciating the drop in temperature. Without stopping to rest they moved up the slope toward the ancient, forgotten path that girdled the hill several hundred feet below the level of the shrine. The chanting of the devout who had gathered in the shrine's broad open courtyard drifted away with the mounting wind and reached the children below only as a soft, indistinguishable murmur. A miracle, the miracle of a man's life, had come to an end in the hours before dawn, and all of Pukmaranpur mourned the event, except for the two children who struggled up the hill in search of a Miracle of their own.

Pamela had no trouble telling when they finally arrived at the abandoned path, for the vegetation changed abruptly. They began moving to their left along its downhill edge, now hearing the mourning chant from within the walls of the shrine above. They could not see the yellow and orange flames which wrapped in shrouds of black sooty smoke, rose from the torches the devout had lighted. The colors stood out in deep relief against the gray and blackening sky. The flames bent over double in gusts of wind and threatened at times to engulf the men who carried the pitch-soaked wood.

The path followed the contour of the land, rising and falling in shallow sagging dips while circling the hill. The circumference of the dome-shaped hill at the level of the forgotten trail was just over seven hundred feet. They had gone slightly less than three hundred feet along the edge of the trail when it came to an abrupt end. They were not more than a hundred yards below the wall that bounded the western face of the shrine. Here the wall was built at the very edge of the plateau. There were no gaps, no breaches, just a solid wall of roughly worked rock faced with a cover of weather and time-worn mortar. Here, too, at the end of the path was a rock jumble, a random pile that could not be seen from above or below.

"What is wrong, Paamela? Why did you shake like that?"

"I saw a cobra, Khoka. It saw us too, but it went under a rock. It was a very big one."

"The *Shadhoobaba* called it away. I told you nothing would hurt us."

The rock jumble was difficult to negotiate. There were endless ridges that rose until they touched the low cover overhead. The children had to crawl over much of it on their hands and knees and, in several places, on their stomachs. Khoka clung to Pamela's ankles and they moved forward in an awkward slithering tandem. In places it was altogether impassable and Pamela constantly sought for easy ways around, but there were few to be found. They were too close to the rocks themselves, many of which were almost buried in rotting vegetation, for Pamela to realize that many of them had been crudely worked. A thousand years earlier an avenue had been made to run through what was now a wasteland of broken stone. It had passed beneath thirteen arches formed by roughly hewn posts and cross members. None of this could Pamela detect as she fought to keep from falling into the endless cracks and crevices in the rubble. The waters of thousands of rain storms had eddied around the ancient structures until the land had slipped away from their foundations, dumping the posts and lintels in upon each other. It was an abandoned world: what had once been of extreme importance to a vanished race was now of account again to two small children made even smaller by the strange nature of their mission.

And suddenly they were upon it — two slanting slabs of stone resting against the hillside. Between them loomed a black cavity nearly fifteen feet high and four feet wide. Pamela stood open-mouthed, staring upward. Across the top of the two guardian slabs a single lintel remained in place. The crudely worked face of a demon god was still visible, leering down at them and defying them to pass. The centuries had done little to soften his stare, for he was the god of the dead and neither he nor his charges acknowledged time.

"We have found it, Paamela! It is here."

"How did you know?"

"By the way you stopped and the way you stand. Don't be afraid, Paamela. I will lead you out of here."

They moved forward cautiously, allowing the guardian posts to slip past them. The leering god receded.

The cave opened almost immediately into an enormous chamber, the far reaches of which were beyond the range of Pamela's vision. The stench was almost as bad as it had been in the *mondir*. For centuries uncounted animals had used the cave when not a man alive shared their knowledge of its existence.

Pamela stood stock still, trying to adjust her eyes to the darkness, but Khoka urged her forward.

"Not too fast, Khoka. I can't see a thing. It's pitch-black in here."

But Khoka was beyond reason. He had reached what he was sure was the end of his odyssey. It had already carried him too far and over too rough a course for him to be deterred by Pamela's hesitation. He pulled her forward, almost lunging to get at the Miracle he was so sure lay ahead.

The events that followed happened too quickly for analysis. Neither child would be able to recall later the sequence exactly as it occurred. They were moving, something else was moving, then Pamela was falling, and her terrified scream rose to fill the cavern and send a thousand bats jerking along their perches.

An animal, a fair-sized animal that neither child could identify, had been just inside the mouth of the cave when they first approached. Startled by the appearance of humans where no humans had ever been before, the four-foot palm civet retreated into the cave to avoid detection. When the children pressed on into the chamber it panicked and raced between them, brushing their legs with its tail as it passed. The rustling it made on the matted dung and the sudden furry contact against their legs caused both children to jump aside in a reflexive movement. The two feet that Pamela moved carried her beyond the edge of a crevice that had existed for five hundred years. The ceiling of another cave farther down the slope had collapsed, the result of slow erosion. She fell seven feet onto a ledge and, although momentarily stunned, was not hurt. She screamed as she fell but it was almost a minute after impact before she was able to call to Khoka. She gasped for breath, trying to control the panic that clutched at her. As for Khoka, the animal brushing against his leg, Pamela's sudden disappearance from his side, and her shrill scream drove him to his knees in the grip of a bewildering terror. He could hear her gasping and he called to her again and again before starting to creep forward on his hands and knees. His fingers slipped over the edge of the drop and he froze, afraid to move now in any direction. He called again and waited, then began sobbing the hopeless lament of a child lost in a nightmare from which he knows the dawn will not rescue him.

Pamela finally managed to bring herself under enough control to assess her predicament. She knew instinctively not to move because even through the blind terror that had accompanied her plunge she had heard rocks falling beyond her, clattering into some deeper chasm.

"Khoka," she called hoarsely, "stay where you are. There's a great hole. You mustn't fall in, too."

"Paamela! Where are you?"

Pamela had landed on her back and could now see Khoka's shadowy outline as he hovered near the edge of the collapsed cave floor above.

"Don't move, Khoka, not even an inch. I'm just below you. Do you understand me?"

Khoka froze and waited. It was difficult to locate sounds in the domed chamber and it took him a minute to grasp what she meant.

"Khoka, you must get help. You must get back to the village or at least to the steps.

"Paamela, I am blind."

The lament rose from the small dark figure huddled on the cave floor and assailed the high vaulted chamber in the bowels of the hill. It sent a thousand bats rustling, and rolled down along the damp walls to rebound again and again until it was broken up by uneven surfaces to be lost in perpetual silence.

"I can't find my way, Paamela. *I can't find my way!*"

Khoka's panic was Pamela's too, for without his help she was doomed. No one, not one living person, knew the cave's location and few if any even believed in its existence.

Slowly, Pamela quieted the terrible feeling of despair that filled her.

"Khoka, listen to me, listen very carefully. Are you listening to me, Khoka?"

"I am listening, Paamela. But I can't find my way. I don't know where I am!"

"Khoka, listen to me, please, because I will die here and so will you unless you get help. Now, listen to what I tell you."

Slowly, carefully, repeating each critical point over and over until she was sure he understood it, Pamela described the moves Khoka would have to make to get out of the cave and back to the steps where she was sure that villagers could still be found. She told him to back up on his hands and knees, to turn to his left and feel his way to the mouth of the cave. She told him as much as she could remember of the rock jumble outside. Once beyond it he would swing to his left again and make his way along the edge of the ancient pathway, moving forward from tree trunk to tree trunk until he came to the stone steps. All of this was predicated, of course, on his not blundering into a crevice . . . or a cobra along the way.

He repeated her instructions and she corrected his mistakes. She tried her best to keep her terror from showing in her voice but was sure that she wasn't doing a very good job of it.

"Khoka. You can do it. Please, Khoka, do it now. Go very slowly."

And then he was gone. Pamela closed her eyes and wept silently. She wasn't at all sure that he would be able to find his way out and even less sure that he would be able to tell the villagers how to get back to where she was. A very frightened little girl lay frozen in the bowels of an ancient cave, her plight the very essence of nightmare. Her distress would have been greater had she known that she shared the chamber with several thousand skeletons. The cave was a long-forgotten burial grotto and nothing more.

Khoka did manage to get to the mouth of the cave. He was met by a strong breeze that was now blowing up the Gamalbuk Valley from the lake far below. As the dank, acidic odor of the cave fell behind him he inched his way out across the rocks, feeling ahead with the palms of his sensitive hands before

shifting his body forward. In places where he sensed
the rocks sloping downward and where he felt he
might pitch forward he sat down and felt ahead with
his bare feet. Twice he fell and badly bruised both
shins and his forehead. A small trickle of blood
seeped down along the outside corner of his left
eye. It took him over an hour to negotiate the shat-
tered, fallen rock, although he had no idea how much
time had elapsed.

As he scrambled over the crest of the last rock he
rolled over on his stomach, clutching with his
fingers, digging for a hold with his bare toes. He let
himself slide downward until he collapsed in a heap
beneath the low canopy of stunted, broad-leafed trees.
He had made so many detours and had had to crawl
back on his own tracks so many times in negotiating
the rocks that he was thoroughly disoriented and
turned to his right instead of his left. He started forward along what he was sure was the edge of the
path. Twice he was thrown backwards off his feet by
branches that slashed cruelly across his face. After
that he stayed on his hands and knees and crept
along for what seemed an eternity. Like the pathway
he was leaving behind him as he moved around the
hill in the wrong direction, Khoka followed the contour of the land. Many times when he thought he
was moving around the hill he was descending
toward the lower slope that opened into an unused

field beyond. The unused field, in turn, ran to the edge of the forest a quarter of a mile south of the old *pilkhana* area at the western edge of the village.

It was two and a half hours after he had left Pamela that Khoka tumbled through the brush at the bottom of the slope. His knees, hands and shins were a mass of cuts and bruises and his face was caked with dirt, blood and tears. He was gasping for breath as he reached high over his head to make certain he could stand without being smacked down to the ground again, as he had been almost every other time he had tried to right himself.

Alone, completely lost, Khoka stood at the edge of the field and called. The wind was now in the first stages of its fury. The weeds and grass around him moaned as they bent double, but there was no one to answer his thin, despairing call for help. He stumbled forward with his hands stretched out before him, calling, *"Amake sahajjo koro!"* again and again, "Help me, help me, help me!"

Khoka had no idea how far he had gone before he finally fell to his knees. He had reached the middle of the abandoned and partially overgrown field before giving up. The edge of the forest was no more than fifty feet away. The village was behind him, beyond the hill, nearly three-quarters of a mile away.

He buried his face in his hands and rocked back

and forth. It was then, just as he was giving up, that he heard it, soft at first, almost swallowed by the wind. But when it came again it was distinct — the low dry grunt that he knew so well. He pulled his hands away from his face and sat in momentary silence, facing toward the jungle. *He has come*, he thought.

"Sarang!" he called, his voice cracking with the effort. "Sarang!"

Slowly Khoka regained his composure and gave the familiar call to which his tiger had always responded. *"Baghh, baghh, baghh,"* he clucked, *"baghh, baghh, baghh."*

The snorting cough came again from the jungle, and then the *ungh-ungh-ungh* of greeting. Khoka couldn't understand why Sarang had not run to him. He stood and moved slowly in the direction from which he thought the sound had come. Again there was the snort, and again the soft *ungh-ungh-ungh*.

As Khoka stumbled forward the bushes parted at the edge of the forest and the tiger inched out into the open. He grunted several times and watched quizzically as the boy wove erratically through the weeds, stumbling, falling, righting himself and falling again. "Sarang!" he called over and over again, *"baghh, baghh, baghh."*

When he was no more than fifteen feet from the tiger, Khoka's foot caught in a tangled root and he fell forward onto his face. He was completely exhausted and as he tried to right himself he sank further into the weeds. His breath came in deep rasping gasps and his mouth was dry and sour. Once again he tried to crawl up onto his knees, only to pitch forward, unable to rise.

The tiger watched his struggles and moved slowly toward him when Khoka came to rest. Twice he circled the boy before moving in to investigate. He had eaten well only three hours before and was neither hungry nor frightened. He was attracted by the strange movements and sounds the boy made and, like most cats, was finding it difficult to resist the temptation to investigate something new and different.

Khoka was on the verge of fainting when he felt the tiger nudge him in the ribs and heard him sniff deeply, and then snort. For the moment he was suspended somewhere between consciousness and coma. But the tiger's touch was too familiar, too much of a stimulus to resist. He rolled over, whispering "Sarang!" and reached up toward the cat, who recoiled and stood off a few feet, eyeing him suspiciously.

"*Baghh*, why don't you come to me?" Khoka pleaded, and slowly extended his hand again. The tiger inched forward and sniffed the bloodstained fingers that reached out for him. Then he licked them, relishing the salty taste of mingled blood and sweat. Khoka held his arm out as the tiger inched forward cautiously, sniffing, licking occasionally, trying to evaluate this new experience.

Finally the tiger stood over Khoka, looking down into his face. Khoka's hand found his foreleg, moved up until it reached the great cat's shoulder. Khoka stroked him gently, speaking softly, as Sarang had always liked him to do.

"Sarang! Thank you for coming. *Amar baghh, amar baghh.*"

The tiger started slightly as Khoka began to sit up but the move did not seem challenging and he held his ground. He had never been this close to a human being before and was fascinated by the smell and the sound of the small boy. As has happened so many other times in history, and as is so well recorded in the literature of the East, a wild tiger came to investigate a human being without malice, with no intent to harm.

Khoka slipped his hand across the tiger's shoulders for support as he stood and in so doing his hand brushed the tiger's neck. His hand froze and slowly worked back through the fur to where the necklace fashioned from Pamela's charm bracelet should have been. And then he knew. A look of elation came over his face as he sank to his knees facing the great cat. He whispered again and again, "A Miracle, a Miracle, a Miracle." A peel of thunder exploded and the storm's first bolt of lightning crackled blindingly into a tree nearby.

And it was then, in the field behind the hill topped by the Buddhist shrine, there where the fires of the sky struck the earth, that Khoka, after seven years of unyielding night, saw his first tiger.

Epilogue

Khoka stood next to his father on the high bank, looking down at the launch as the lines were cast off. He could see Pamela standing half hidden behind a crate, trying to mask her tears.

Khoka felt that he must not cry, for now he was twelve and training with his father to become a *phandi*. Already he was riding out with Ma on Sikander and soon he would be a *mahout*. He would be helping to carry forward the work that Glenn had started and which had become a way of life in Pukmaranpur. Such men do not cry.

Off to the side four elephants stood facing the river. Bolo Bahadur, Sikander, Begam Bahar and the rented cow Meernah Prue, her pregnancy far advanced, stood in a well-ordered row. Each *mahout* in turn gave the command and the four heads lifted as trunks coiled back to rest on the four broad brows. Khoka looked along the line of elephants, and then, with pride, up at his father. It is beautiful, he thought, beautiful to be the son of a *bor phandi*, beautiful to know elephants and to be alive in a place like Pukmaranpur.

So much had happened since the day when he had first heard that foreigners had come to live in the village. First came Pamela, then Prince, then Sarang, and the flight through the forest in search of the *Shadhoobaba* from whom his faith had come. Then the cave and Pamela's fall and the wild tiger who had given him the Miracle he had believed in with all his heart and soul. Then the struggle through the storm that crashed around him and drove the tiger back into the forest, and finally his reaching the lodge and collapsing at Liz's feet as she screamed for Glenn. He remembered, too, the return to the cave just as night was falling, and Pamela's rescue.

So much had happened.

And the mysteries. The story that had reached the village that on the day of the terrible storm, the day of the Miracle, the great *mondir* to the north had collapsed inward with a terrible roar. Finally, the mystery of Sarang, who had not been seen nor heard since Khoka regained his sight.

Khoka gazed up at his father, who was even taller and stronger than he had pictured him. Satwyne held his shoulder tightly.

Slowly Khoka raised his hand and waved to Pamela, and to Liz and Glenn, who stood at the rail of the launch as it slipped away from the bank into the current. He could see the tears streaming down Pamela's cheeks as the launch turned downriver. So much had happened. So much in the course of one short year.

Glenn turned to Liz.

"We're going home, honey."

Liz, who had given up her plan to adopt Khoka once his sight returned, looked up at her husband. She moved closer to him.

"Are we, Glenn? I wonder. I wonder where home is."

About This Book . . .

As far as I know the village of Pukmaranpur does not exist, and no one seems to know where Khoka really came from. Perhaps he is just an imaginary figure, one more product of tropical Asia's boundless capacity for creating and sustaining stories and legends.

While both Khoka and Pukmaranpur *may* be fictional, the peoples of the Chittagong Hill Tracts are not. To the good citizens of the Mugg village of Chittmaran just across the Karnaphuli River from the Kaptai Road who taught me to eat the mango and who showed me how a wild elephant becomes a working companion of man, I owe my thanks. To M. A. Khan and Ata-ur Rahman Khan of Dacca, to A. Waheed Khawaja and Ahmedullah Noor of Chittagong, and Mohammed Asrar of Karachi, who gave me so much of their own valuable time in order that I might come to know and understand East Pakistan, I shall be forever grateful. In all my travels — and I consider myself among the most fortunate of men because they have been extensive — I have never known friendlier or more hospitable people. I arrived in their land alone and a stranger, but within days I had access to everyone and everything any writer could ever hope for in pursuit of a story. I cannot imagine people giving more willingly or completely of themselves or their affection, not to mention such numerous matters as transport, food, advice and good cheer.

And then there were Ivan Tors and Ralph Helfer of Africa, U.S.A. There, in their private Eden not far from the edge of the great California desert, they introduced me to the real-life Sarang. How difficult it was to believe. The magic they had wrought! Sarang probably can't walk a tightrope, and it is certain that neither Ivan nor Ralph has ever asked him to jump through a flaming hoop, for he is no circus animal brutalized out of his dignity and forced to perform degrading tricks. In all of his original dignity, the real Sarang, as he lives today, is five hundred pounds of majesty, a magnificent Bengal tiger who lives among men because he loves them, in return for their love for him. There are no guns there, and Sarang has never been prodded with a chair, intimidated with a whip or forced into some ugly, perverted obedience. He walks with men, unchained and unafraid, as their companion and as their friend, as he and they choose it to be. I have hugged Sarang, I have felt his whiskers against my cheek, and I have heard him purr his contentment. It is because of Sarang, as he exists today, that I tend, perhaps, to think that Khoka, too, was once real. But then, I'll never know for sure. I wonder if it really matters.

Roger Caras